Selah:סלה

The Book of Books Chronicles

This Book is dedicated to my three heart beats and reasons for being: Gabrielle, Isabella, and Benjamin. Everything I do is for you.

"And he took up his parable and said—Enoch a righteous man, whose eyes were opened by God, saw the vision of the Holy One in the heavens, which the angels showed me, and from them I heard everything, and from them I understood as I saw, but not for this generation, but for a remote one which is to come."

The Book of Enoch

Prologue

The cool desert wind blew softly across the bronze skin of the tall man. The wind was leading him, always leading him. Had he company with him, they would not have felt the wind, for the air didn't move. Nothing rustled, shifted, or moved, but the lone man felt it, saw it. His face was set in lines of determination, his shoulders proud, and his steps sure. In the darkness of the night, he had no fear, and though there was barely any light, he was surefooted. For there are those who walk by sight, and those who walk by faith. This man was part of the latter group.

His face wasn't a friendly face by any means. It was a face older than time, with eyes filled with wisdom. Eyes that have seen more than any ordinary man could comprehend. When people of the desert met him for the first time, they all unconsciously bowed to him, and called him Adon or Sayyid, a custom long since lost from these parts of the world. For change is inevitable and worlds are constantly changing, forming, evolving. Nothing lasts forever under Heaven. But this desert—the bedrock of creation—this desert always remembers. Throughout the years, he has been called by many titles—Master, Teacher, Friend. He has been a father, soldier, king, and lived so many lives. Yet his task has always remained the same—to teach, protect, and initiate those among the Beni Adam who were chosen for a special task. This time, he would find the one who can read the *Sefer Ha-Sefarim*, the Book of Books.

This time would be different, the *Ruach Ha-Elohim*, God's Breath, was leading him out of the desert. He would have to travel to a land far away from Tsion, to a land of babbling tongues. It wasn't his first journey to foreign lands. He had found Dani-El in such a place a long time ago. Dani-El and his three friends, strangers in a strange land. But this one would require him crossing the waters and going further than he has ever been from Tsion. He would do it of course, because he walked with Elohim, and was always faithful.

When he reached the top of the dune, he paused and looked behind him before crossing the valley that would lead him into the crowded city. His eyes searched over the dunes, seeing more than human eyes could see. He knew that if another stood there and looked, all they would see was sand. The days of the *Chozim*, the *Navim*, were gone. The people in The Book long since stolen away from this land. And the land mourned her children, all of Heaven mourned the loss of those children written of in the Book.

Which was why, after generations, he was back. The man who never died but was taken by Elohim—the teacher of the sages, who initiates the *Tzaddikim*, the *Chozim*, those in the Order. He would travel and locate his charge— a youth to be initiated. For the words needed to be spoken. He took some time to think about his last charge, his last initiate, and he sighed. How lost they had been back then, those written in the Book. They stopped hearing the voice of their *Eloah* and stopped listening to the *Navim* sent to them by their Creator. And they were even more lost now—worshiping false gods, praying to gods whose names their fathers never knew. They had been stolen, and were lost. Their language, their land, all gone. And now they were on the verge of causing the end of all creation. He shook his head, for he had no time for recollections or grief. He had a task to perform for Elyon.

He continued walking down the dune, took the last step from desert sand to the dry earth of the valley and stood on the *adamah,* the ground. How long had it been since he felt solid ground beneath his feet? With shoulder squared, he walked with faith. He had no bags, no identification or money, he knew whatever he needed it would be provided. It had always been this way. He spoke all languages, knew all customs. The knowledge simply came, as it always did. He walked out of the desert making his way to a land called New York, to find a young man named Selah—a boy chosen to read the *Sefer Ha-Sefarim*.

"*Maktub*." He whispered into the wind. *It is written.* And with that, he walked back into the world of man.

Chapter One

His first memory was of pain. He was four years old and they were on their way home from a party, he and his mother. He didn't really remember her face, only that she smelled of lavender. To this day, the smell of lavender makes him want to cry. His mother lost control of the car, and they dived into a ditch. He was told it had been a miracle that he survived. His mother hadn't. He spent three days alone trapped in that ditch, cold, and hungry, before a truck driver miraculously saw the car. The driver would later tell the highway patrol that he had no reason to look into that ditch but felt compelled to do so.

No one knew what caused the accident. His mother wasn't a drinker and had no known medical conditions. It wasn't the first time in his life that tragedy came for him. He was born during the early hours of a warm August morning, or at least that is the guess of the medical staff of Mount Sinai Hospital where he was taken after being found near a dumpster. They never found the woman who had left him wrapped in a towel, shoved amongst the refuse. He was found on a windy day by a nurse who worked at the hospital. The harried nurse was on her way to work when she heard a baby crying. The nurse would later explain how strange it had been, how serendipitous it felt that day when she heard him. After all, her headphones had been on pretty high and the wind was blowing fiercely. In her most fanciful moments, she would tell friends that the wind carried his cries to her.

The nurse was Sharon Jacobi, daughter of Solomon Jacobi, and she would adopt the baby she found in the dumpster. She couldn't explain her reasoning. She was a woman in her late forties looking forward to retiring, and a widow, but all she knew was that he was hers. "Finders keepers," she had said with a smile. Her father Solomon Jacobi was a devout Jewish scholar whom she adored and moved in with after the death of her husband. Her mother passed away when she was very young. The two Jacobis were each other's sole comfort in this world. When she told the old man that she was adopting an infant, he simply shrugged and said, "Hashem provides." That's what he always said, "Hashem provides."

Solomon Jacobi was a kind man who raised his daughter to be compassionate and giving. He was called Rabbi by everyone in their Brooklyn neighborhood, though he was never in any Yeshiva and wasn't a member of a synagogue. Solomon Jacobi agreed with Karl Marx's observation that religion was indeed the opiate of the masses. As such, he taught his daughter to have an open mind to all cultures and to read the Torah. "If you need to know something," he would say "Hashem will send you the answer." He taught religious studies at Queens College, until he retired. The old man spent his time after retirement having long conversations with his friends. He was in contact with many of his old students, for once a teacher, always a teacher. When, at the hospital, they had placed the baby in his arms, he had smiled. A simple and sweet smile of recognition. He looked up at his daughter and said, "Selah," and so they named him. Solomon was eighty years old when his daughter died and left him the sole guardian of a scared little boy. Through sheer will he lasted another five years before he was taken to sleep with his ancestors. Selah was ten years old when he became a ward of the City of New York, and fifteen, when his life completely changed.

Selah hated the walks back to the apartment. It was not his home—that would be the wrong word for the place where he was currently residing until he was either transferred or turned eighteen. Whichever came first. In the past five years, he had lost count of the number of "homes" he was placed in. His case worker was clueless as to why his placements weren't working out. Selah wasn't a troublemaker. In fact, by anyone's description, he was a quiet boy, who mostly kept to himself. He had smooth brown skin, soft wooly hair, and a steady calm disposition that unsettled most adults.

There was something about him that seemed different, though no one could pinpoint what it was. His foster parents could never really give a good reason why they wanted a different placement, only that they were not the right "fit." Selah himself couldn't understand what it was about him that made people feel vulnerable or uncomfortable. Once, not long in the foster care system, he heard one of the foster parents arguing. He remembers the wife telling her husband that it was his eyes. "He looks at you like he knows you; he knows all the shit you ever did, and he is disappointed in you." He wasn't even sure what that meant, but since she was always drunk, it was safe to say that she probably didn't know what she meant either.

His stride became slower as he got closer to the building where his current foster parents lived. They were a nice enough couple, the McCullens. Tanya was a teacher— she taught third grade at P.S 115 in Queens. She hated the commute and had been looking for a transfer for years. Jackson McCullen was a mechanic at a local shop. He walked to work, and this was a point of contention between them since Tanya was constantly angry about her husband's good fortune and took every opportunity to remind him that he didn't know how hard her life was. Ms. McCullen was perpetually aggravated by everyone. Selah suspected that the person she was the angriest with was herself. She seemed disappointed in her life and, as a result, resolved not to enjoy it and wouldn't let anyone enjoy theirs in her presence.

He stopped completely when he saw the familiar Honda Accord parked in front of the building. "Shit!" he whispered, because he knew what that meant. He would be meeting his new Mom and Dad by the end of the week.

Lisa Johnson had been Selah' s case worker since he was five years old, after he was placed with his adoptive grandfather. It took a lot of fancy talk on her part to get the court to approve placing a five-year-old boy in the care of an eighty-year-old man. Solomon had loved the boy, and Selah likewise. He had lost his mother, and the courts agreed that as long as she kept an eye on them, he could stay with Solomon. Though she knew it would not, could not, be for too long. It broke her heart when she had to put him in the system. Sitting in the McCullens's living room, she wondered how many times she would have to have this conversation with these damn people.

"What exactly has Selah done that you are requesting a change in placement?"

"It's not that he has done anything," Jackson McCullen stammered, "It's just..."

"Not a good fit" the words came from the doorway where Selah stood. There was no anger in his voice, just resignation. For some reason, that was even worse. She looked at the faces of the McCullens. They would not make eye contact with the boy. For the hundredth time she wondered "what is it about him?" Truth is she loved Selah. Not just because he was on her caseload. There was just something about him—a stoicism far too developed for someone so young, a knowing, a maturity not found in many adults.

Selah was a tall, good-looking boy, and she had to force herself not to touch his hair every time she saw him. It wasn't his physical appearance that made him stand out, it was his presence. That was the word for it, the boy had *presence*. Even with adults and authority figures who he should have been intimidated by, he never was, at least none that you could see. There was a certain power, like you were standing in front of a boy king. It felt as though you should be listening to him and not the other way around. It was very unsettling, even for her. However, unlike the others, Lisa loved the boy.

"Selah!" She smiled and stood to greet him. "I stopped by to speak to the McCullens..." she started but paused when he looked at her. She took a breath and sighed. A while ago, he made her promise never to lie to him. So today she decided that his trust meant more to her than protocol.

"The McCullens have requested that you be placed somewhere else. I have asked them to give me three days, or until the end of the week, to find you a suitable placement. You know the drill," she said and shrugged.

The couple exchanged surprised looks, not expecting her to be so frank with the kid. They were anticipating tears, anger, and accusations. Instead, Selah nodded to the adults. Accepting his fate, trusting. He wasn't sure what he trusted. He trusted Ms. Johnson for sure; she had always been good to him. Besides his mother and grandfather, she was the only person that he had ever cared about. More than Ms. Johnson, Selah trusted in an unknown and unseen source. A source whose guiding hand he had felt all his life. An unseen presence, he could not explain or describe in words. He felt it. All his life, standing over his shoulder. Watching him, weighing him. He wasn't sure, maybe he was crazy.

The awkward silence stretched and was broken by Mrs. McCullen. "It's not you, Selah, it's just that we got lots going on, and we talked and really want to start our own family, and we are not sure if we are going to take in foster kids anymore. I'm sure you understand." She was lying, they all knew it. Again, Selah nodded, understanding her need to lie, to justify what she herself could not understand.

Selah didn't blame her, or the other families, group home, and even other children, who found him unsettling. He wasn't sure what it was, but there was something. When he was twelve, Ms. Johnson took him to a doctor and had him evaluated for Asperger's. She thought it might be the reason he had a hard time connecting with others. It wasn't Asperger's, she knew that as well, but had to quantify or label "the difference" in him. Selah was simply different. Always had been, always will be. He knew with the certainty of the tides that he had an awesome, terrible purpose. Something far beyond his imagination. He didn't know when or how, but he knew his life would not follow an ordinary course. So, he watched, he listened, he learned, and he waited.

"Come, we will have dinner together, my treat." Lisa grabbed her purse, and said goodbye to the McCullens, feeling less than generous towards the couple. She took Selah's arm and the two of them walked out of the apartment.

"So, what'll it be? McDonald's, Chinese?" She smiled at the boy. He smiled back, knowing she was trying to do her best to normalize his situation. And he loved her for the effort. "Chinese," he said. "We could walk there; the weather is nice." The two of them started walking the two blocks to the Golden Wok Chinese Restaurant. He knew she had more to say, otherwise she would have left. So, he braced himself, and with resignation let her lead them down the block.

"It's not your fault you know."

She looked up from her menu and smiled, "You are stealing my lines, kid. Shouldn't I be saying this to you?" They were sitting at the restaurant as she tried to prolong the inevitable. Selah sighed and put his menu down, he already knew what he was going to order.

"This place lasted longer than the others." He never called them "home"; he had lost his home long ago.

"I asked them to give me a few days, but I don't know. Placements in homes are hard ... it might have to be a group home. I know you don't like them. But...."

"It's not your fault," he repeated, because she needed to hear it and he needed to say it.

"It's not yours either. I know I keep making promises and breaking them. So, this time I won't say anything other than to say, I will find you a new place. I am so sorry, Selah."

"I know you are. I know you try to do your best. I—" but he stopped because he couldn't find the words to comfort either one of them.

"Well, then let's eat, uh?"

After dinner, the two figures walked back to the apartment building where the boy would be spending the next few days. As they walked, Selah looked at the neighborhood—taking mental pictures, remembering the people he met while living here and the things that they taught him. Solomon would tell him, "Everyone you meet has a story, Selah, and they should be remembered." He missed the old man, the steadiest influence in his life up to this point. He tried not to be afraid, but fear came to him anyway, like an uninvited guest.

As they drew closer to the main door to the building, he felt the wind. At first just a slight breeze, barely ruffling his shirt, but then the wind became more persistent. Almost like it was trying to get his attention. On a regular night, to a regular boy, the wind would have gone unnoticed. But not on this night, and not by this boy. Because, while the wind was strong enough that he had to push against it, nothing moved. Branches didn't sway, leaves didn't ruffle, nothing moved. It seemed the wind had selected only him for this special honor.

Confused, Selah turned to look at Ms. Johnson. Her hair, clothes, were not moving and she didn't seem to be in any way encumbered by the sensation of the wind. Selah remembered sitting in the park with Solomon many years ago on a cool autumn day, watching the wind blow through the leaves. The old man loved sitting in the park.

"Why do you love the wind so much?"

"Ah," said the old man, "before anything was created, the *Ruach* was present. It was the only thing in this realm that was able to sing in worship of the Most High," Solomon said with a secret smile. But that was so long ago, and Solomon was not here to enjoy this wind.

All of Selah's senses were awakened by the sensation of the wind. He could not explain it or comprehend exactly what was happening. But something was about to happen, something amazing.

"Selah?" He turned to look at his caseworker.

"Are you alright? You have this strange look on your face."

"Yeah, yeah. Just tired. I am going in now, thanks for dinner."

"Well, I can walk you inside," she said.

"N- No, it's cool. I got it from here. Besides, it's getting late. And I am the man, let me walk you to your car."

He hurried her to her car and, on impulse, pulled her into a hug. He had never intentionally shown her any physical sign of affection. At first, she was taken aback by the display, then she returned the embrace. "Thank you," he said with feeling. "You have been good to me; I will never forget that."

With a nervous laugh, she pulled back to look at his face. "Now hold on, why does this sound like you are trying to say goodbye? I will see you soon."

The young man smiled, "Yeah I know. I just wanted to say thank you."

"You're welcome," she said. And on impulse, because this seemed to be a night of firsts, she kissed his cheek. "You are a good boy Selah." Resigned more than ever to find him a good home, she got in her car. With one last look at the boy, she waved and left.

Alone in the parking lot, Selah stood quietly in the dark, waiting for what he wasn't really sure. The wind stopped blowing. After a few more minutes when nothing happened, Selah exhaled. He didn't even notice he had been holding his breath. Feeling as though he had been holding his breath for five years now, he shook his head, disappointment hitting him. He wasn't sure what he was expecting would happen. His heart was hurting, and this being a night of firsts, tears gathered in his eyes. Head down, shoulders dropped, the young man resigned himself to his course and started walking back towards the front of the building.

"Oseh Shalom bi- roma, Hu yasseh shalom Aleicha, Ben Adam" May He who makes peace in high places, make peace upon you, Son of Man. The voice came out of the night from the eastside of the building. From the corner of the building, a man walked out of the shadows. No, not a man, he was far more than that. How he knew this he could not explain, but Selah knew this was the moment he had been waiting for.

"Aleicha shalom," Selah answered, *peace be upon you*. The answer came without him thinking about it. It was the response that his grandfather would give his friends when they would come to visit them at their apartment.

"Why are you downtrodden, Ben Adam, don't you know? Before the words leave your heart, and pass through your lips, Heaven has already answered you. All you have to do is have faith and wait for the answer."

"Who are you?" Selah asked, with his heart stuck in his throat.

"Who I am isn't as important as who you are," he answered.

"Who do you think I am?" There was longing and sadness in the question. The man walked further out of the darkness. "You are who you have always been, who you will

17

always be, regardless of your situation or circumstances. But now, it is more important than ever that you become."

"Become what? Please, I—" He couldn't find the words to explain what he was asking the stranger. So, instead, he repeated, "Who are you?"

When all he received was a measuring look from the stranger, he offered, "My name is Selah."

The stranger smiled. "I have been called many names by many people over the years. You can call me Enoch Ben Yared."

"Did the strange wind bring you?" This was a weird question, but it was turning out to be a weird night.

"Yes, the *Ruach* leads and I follow."

"I don't understand. It leads you? Where do you come from? Why are you here?" Selah felt strangely comfortable with the man. No, not comfortable, the man felt familiar somehow. He was wearing dark pants and a long shirt. The lower half of his face was obscured by a beard. His clothing and speech sounded Middle Eastern like Muhammad, the kind owner of the corner store where Selah would buy his breakfast. His accent, while Middle Eastern, was more lyrical though. It was beautiful and peaceful. Selah couldn't determine his age. While his hair had touches of gray at the temple, his face was unlined.

"I am here because you are here," he answered.

"Me?"

"Yes, you—" Abruptly Enoch turned to face a dark corner of the building. Selah had been fascinated and excited at meeting the man but now, for the first time on this strange night, he felt apprehension. From the shadows a figure emerged. Tall, taller than Enoch, broad and menacing. The shadow congealed and a man appeared. Selah gasped; now terror had set in. For this was no mere human either, of that he was sure. The figure started towards them. "Do not run." Enoch muttered.

"Remember, Man was given dominion over the earth, Ben Adam. Those who enter your realm must answer to your command." He hurriedly supplied. He hadn't had enough time to speak with the boy, Enoch thought, but he could say no more to him now. No one can escape the Laws.

Frozen in place by fear, Selah could only whimper, "Who is that?" though, *what* may be more appropriate.

"Your tsar," answered Enoch, resigned to the imminent confrontation. Selah knew that word. It was a Hebrew word meaning adversary or opponent.

"I see you found the boy." His voice was mocking, and cruelly indifferent. He looked Selah over, weighing him.

You must know his name, Enoch thought to himself, projecting his own energy onto Selah, trying to keep the boy calm. *You cannot fight something you do not know.* But he could not speak to the boy, because the Laws must be obeyed. The Laws were written long before the gods created man, the Laws which kept the world in balance. No one was above the Laws.

"Who are you? What is your name?" whispered Selah, scared beyond anything he had ever experienced in his young life. He remembered all those fairy tales that involved finding out the name of the monster, knowing that this was much worse than *Rumpelstiltskin*. He knew this was not a simple conversation. That, somehow, his very life depended on his interaction with these strangers. He wasn't even sure why he felt the need to know this person's name. He knew it was a vital piece of information. ʼ

"Why do you ask?"

Why do you ask? His answer struck Selah as odd. And the tone he used seemed contrived. The thought calmed him and brought with it a long-forgotten memory. Many years prior, Selah would spend his afternoons with Solomon studying the Torah. Solomon didn't have many pleasures in this world, but one thing the old man loved was spending time with his only grandson and best friend, reading from the

Torah. On one such occasion he read the story of Yaqoob wrestling with an angel. Always a wonderful storyteller, Solomon had the boy enraptured by the story of a man's fight with a god. He paused in the middle of the story when Yaqoob asked the god/angel for his name. The god/angel asks Yaqoob, "Why do you ask?"

Solomon had turned his shrewd eyes and asked the boy, "Do you see Yaqoob's mistake?"

"No, what did he do wrong?" asked Selah.

"Hashem gave man dominion over the mortal realm. He should have commanded him to tell him his name. Then the angel would have blessed him and healed him and Yaqoob would not have spent his life walking with a limp. He walked with a limp for the rest of his life, you know. You would not make such a mistake, would you?"

"No," said the young boy, smiling.

Now the young man stood in the dark with two men, knowing that his response was just as important as the one from Yaqoob. With his heart ready to gallop out of his chest, the young boy replied, "I- I am not asking you. I command you to tell me your name."

Everything stood still. Even the trees had taken a breath and held it. All the Universe was facing this scene in the parking lot of a building in a city, where a young man took a stand in a fight older than thought, time, and space. The man froze; Enoch smiled ever so slightly.

The man turned to look at Enoch with an accusatory stare. "I follow the Laws," said Enoch, "I gave him no instruction, other than what was allowed."

The man then replied, "I am Tsar-El."

Knowing he had somehow managed to survive this night, and wanting nothing more than to walk away, Selah said, "Then leave, your business is done here." Tsar-El looked at the boy and inhaled a long breath. "Ah! Yes, this will be a fight after all. *Shalom Aleicha,* Ben Adam."

"*Aleicha Shalom*," replied Selah instinctively. With that Tsar-El walked back into the shadows and was gone. Bending over, breath wheezing out of his lungs, Selah could not fight the chills that came all over him.

"Easy, Ben Adam, easy. One breath at a time."

"I- I don't—" He wasn't sure what he wanted to say, so he concentrated on breathing instead. Once he felt calmer, he turned and asked, "Who or what was that?"

"I have answered that question. He is your adversary."

"Where did he come from?"

"He has always been with you, just as your guide has always been with you. It is the Universal Law. There is a duality in the universe. There can be no light without darkness, no love without hate, no good without evil."

"Does that make you my guardian angel?"

A small smile played on Enoch's face. "No, not your 'guardian angel' as you say. I am your teacher, should you choose it."

"I have a choice?" asked Selah.

"There is always a choice, Ben Adam,'" Enoch replied.

"What would have happened if I hadn't gotten his name?"

"You would have been at a disadvantage in this fight."

"Fight?" After a while, he asked, "Why was he opposing me? Why was he here? What did I do for him to hate me?" Selah was confused, and a little angry. He was hoping this night, meeting this stranger would bring clarity, but instead he was feeling even more confused.

"Hate? He does not hate you. An adversary opposes you. He has a task as I do, as all creation does. He performs his task as commanded. Hate has nothing to do with it. He is subject to the Laws in the same way as all creation."

"Laws? The Torah? You read the Torah?"

"As above, so below," he replied.

"That means I won. Did I win the fight?"

"You did well, but no, you didn't win. You entered the fight."

"Is this why I am different, why I have always felt...set apart?"

"Yes. That which is chosen must be removed from the rest."

"Now what, what am I being chosen for?"

"You are chosen from the Beni Adam to read the Book. All of creation depends on it."

"Okay. Where is this Book? Let me read it. Is it in Hebrew? I can read it a little. Solomon taught me."

"Yes, the old man did well with you. But no, the Book is not with me. Only you can find the Book."

"Alright, then where do we look?"

"It is far more complicated than that. When you are ready, the Book will call you. In the meantime, I must get you away from here."

With that Enoch started walking towards the entrance of the building. Selah hurried after him, giving the corner where Tsar-El vanished one last apprehensive look.

"Hold up, where are we going?" Everything was happening too fast. Selah needed a minute to gather his thoughts.

Enoch asked the boy gently, "Do you wish to stay? Are you attached to someone here?" This was the hardest part. Taking them away from those their hearts longed for.

Thinking of Ms. Johnson, Selah hesitated. Then the realization came to him that soon she would not be able to help him. He would age out of the system, or worse, he might be removed from her caseload. What would he do then? He wasn't a pessimist or a cynic, but he knew there was only so much Ms. Johnson could do for him. She was not his family or his home. He didn't have one anymore. "No...I have no attachments here."

When they got to the entrance of the building, while searching for his key, Selah asked again, "Where are we going?"

"Tsion."

Selah froze. "Zion is real, it's a real actual place?" Selah asked with wonder. "Why Zion?"

"Because, יהוה *will inscribe in the register of people that each was born there...*Selah."

"Psalm 87." Selah smiled at the look of surprise on Enoch's face.

"Ah! Yes, your grandfather has done well with you." Enoch said, pleased with the boy. "We must hurry, we have already spent enough time here. Dawn will bring its own challenges."

Getting into the elevator, a thought occurred to Selah. "You said there is a duality in the universe. That everything has its opposite. In this fight, am I the good guy?"

Enoch hesitated, searching for an answer that would suffice without overwhelming the boy. After a while he said, "In its simplest form, yes, you are the 'good guy'."

"Then who is the bad guy? Is he my enemy?"

"I do not know who he is, or where. But there will be an opposing force to you, one who will try to destroy you. But he too will be subject to the Law and I will teach you to master the Law.

Chapter Two

The apartment was a three-floor walkup with well-lit hallways. It had a superintendent who took great pride in his building. Selah felt an unexpected pang when he realized he was actually going to miss this place. He had been placed in six foster homes prior to this one; the McCullens were his seventh set of foster parents. Selah was always polite and made sure he kept his space clean. He worked very hard at being the perfect guest. It seemed to him that his hosts felt aggravated by his conscientiousness, more so than if he had been rude and disobedient. He shook his head, scattering those thoughts as he entered the apartment; the past was no longer important, it was the future that he cared about.

The McCullens must have gone to their room to avoid having to speak to him, he thought, which would make it easier for him to leave. Once in his room, he turned to observe Enoch, while he in turn observed Selah.

"What?" asked Selah.

Enoch looked around at the almost empty room. It looked unoccupied. The empty room said more about the boy than if it had been covered in memorabilia and junk, the way one would expect a young man's room to be.

"I was going to instruct you to take only the most valuable items with you, but I see it will not be necessary."

Selah walked towards the dresser and pulled out a black backpack, one of the strong utility types, and started to pack his things. He took most of his clothes—he didn't have much anyway—his grandfather's Bible, and his mother's picture. Taking a deep breath, he turned to Enoch.

"Are you ready?" Enoch asked.

Selah understood that he wasn't asking him a simple question. Enoch was inquiring not only about his general sense of preparedness for the trip, but rather his mental state. Truth is, he was scared. Selah had never been more afraid, but at the same time, he had never felt this sense of ... being present. For most of his life, he had felt like an understudy in a play. He knew all the lines, knew the queues, but was just a shadow backstage, watching everyone else play their parts, waiting his turn. This was his turn, he was center stage, under the lights. He wouldn't let fear take that away from him, not now that he was so close to ... he wasn't sure what, but something.

He squared his shoulders, lifted his chin, took a breath, and nodded. Enoch looked at the boy, seeing more than Selah could have imagined, and after what felt like an eternity, he mirrored Selah's gesture.

"Come, we must be on our way." The two travelers silently left the apartment. The younger following the older, both walking purposefully towards the future that awaited them.

They walked silently for a few blocks, not because Selah didn't have any questions, but rather because Enoch didn't seem the type to give credence to inane chit chat.
When he turned left towards the corner, Selah said, "The train station is the other way."

"We are not heading towards the train, we need provisions, transportation, and somewhere to rest for the night. This has been an eventful evening; the mind needs rest as much as the body does."

Perplexed, Selah asked, "Then why didn't we stay at the McCullens's for the night? They don't check my room."

Enoch stopped walking and turned towards him. "Why would you wish to stay there? You were never welcome; one does not stay where one is not welcome." He turned and kept walking, stopping in front of the One Stop

Delicatessen. He looked up at the sign like he was listening for something or trying to decipher the hidden meaning in the name of the deli. Having finally made up his mind, he turned to his charge, "Come." Shaking his head at the odd behavior, Selah followed.

The first time Selah met Muhammad Ibn Baqarah, he liked him on contact. One would think that a boy raised by a Jew may feel some reticence about befriending a Muslim man, but he didn't. He had been living with the McCullens for a few days, and he was feeling homesick and lonely. He had decided to take a walk and explore the neighborhood. He had entered the store, not with the intention of buying anything but mostly because it was something to do. Muhammad was standing behind the counter reading a foreign newspaper and drinking coffee. When he looked up, the two of them made eye contact. He had kind eyes, so Selah mumbled, "*Salam alaikum.*"

"*Alaikum Salam,*" replied Muhammad with a smile and lowered his paper to pay closer attention to his young patron.

"You are new to the neighborhood?"

"Yes, I was just looking around, you know. Getting used to the place."

"What is your name, young man?"

"Selah Jacobi, pleased to meet you."

"The pleasure, I think, will be mine, young one."

The two started an unlikely friendship. Every morning Selah would stop by the store on his way to school to get breakfast; he preferred eating with Mr. Muhamad than with the McCullens. After school he would stop on his way home and regale Mr. Muhammad with the goings-on at an inner-city high school. Mr. Muhammad would ask him questions about his day, and make sure he had a snack. He learned a lot about his young friend. He knew that Selah felt awkward and out of place. What he didn't understand was why such a special person would want to be like everyone else.

The tinkling of the door alerted Muhammad to their presence. Turning, he smiled when he saw the boy. "Salam alai—" The words stayed trapped in his throat when he saw the man standing next to his friend. For a few minutes, the older man looked transfixed, with a look of pure joy and wonder. It was the look of a man witnessing the culmination of all his dreams.

Stopping a few steps in front of him, Enoch greeted him as it was written. *"Bismillah Ar- Rahman Ar- Rahim"* *In the name of Allah The Beneficent, the Merciful.*
Muhammad replied, *"Al hamdu Lillahi Rabbi Al- Alamina, Maliki yawmi ad- din." Praise be to the Lord of the Worlds, Master of the Day of Judgement.*

Then both men said, *"Iyyaka Na budu wa Iyyaka Nasta inu." Thee alone we worship, and thee alone we implore for help.*

Selah had never seen the look on Mr. Muhammad's face on another adult. That look was reserved for small children on Christmas morning who had just received every item on their list. "Mr. Muhammad." Selah said with concern. Bowing at the waist, Muhammad said, *"Sayyid,* if I have found favor in your eyes, please do not pass your servant by. Let me give you something to eat and house you for the night. All that I have, I give freely." Enoch walked to Muhammad and the two men exchanged elaborate hand signals then embraced each other.

"Do as you have said Muhammad Ibn Baqarah," replied Enoch.

Muhammad bowed once again then turned to face Selah. *"Habibi,* I knew meeting you was fortunate, I didn't realize just how fortunate it would turn out to be." Then he walked towards the back of the store. At the back of the store was a staircase that led to the apartments upstairs where Muhammad and his family lived.

Selah often wondered how they spent their time away from the store. In all honesty, Muhammad was always in the store, and Selah often wondered if it allowed him to have any kind of life. Muhammad and his wife Amatul had four children, all girls. They had great expectations for their daughters. Selah had once asked him about having only female children since having a son to carry the family name was so important in Islam. Muhammad had said, "The Qur'an teaches us 'But whosoever does deeds of righteousness be it male or female, then who shall enter Paradise and shall not be treated unjustly even so much as the grove in a date-stone' as long as they are good people, I am most blessed with my daughters."

They spent many afternoons talking about life and love. Mr. Muhammad started teaching him the Qur'an and answering Selah's questions. It was the most peaceful time that Selah had spent in this neighborhood. He thought he knew Mr. Muhamad, but now seeing him with Enoch, seeing the way he responded, as if he knew Enoch, led Selah to think of the serendipitous nature of their relationship.

"Follow me," said Muhammad. When he reached the top of the staircase which would lead them to the apartment's living area, Muhammad called out in Arabic to the women upstairs. Selah had learned a few words but could barely make out any of what he said. At the women's response to his inquiry, Muhammad waved the two travelers inside his home.

"Please come in,'" he gestured, as the two of them crossed the threshold. The apartment was beautiful, with warm colors and comfortable furniture. It gave the guests an instant feeling of welcome. Selah felt his shoulders relax; he hadn't been aware of them being tight until that moment. The five women were standing in the center of the room, obviously caught off guard by the change in routines. After a few words with his family, Muhammad guided them to the dining area, where the evening meal was being laid out.

"I will call Yusuf to close the store and will return shortly." Once again, he bowed to Enoch before leaving the room. The women busied themselves with setting up the meal with great fanfare, in the way one would if they were receiving honored guests. Selah figured it was a natural part of their customs. Mr. Muhammad had once told him that hospitality was one of the cornerstones of Islam. He had asked why that was the case, "The Prophet teaches us: *Whoever believes in Allah and the last day should be hospitable with his or her guests,* so you make sure you honor your guest, *Habibi*," he had replied. Mr. Muhammad had been the best part of living with the McCullens; Selah didn't realize how lucky he had been to have made such a friend until now. Muhammad didn't ask any questions, and asking nothing in return, had opened his home to him. Selah felt humbled and safe. Amatul returned and seated them at the table, with Enoch seated as the guest of honor.

Seated across Enoch, Selah wondered about the earlier interaction between the two men. He considered his words, and then asked, "How do you know Mr. Muhammad?"

"I have never met your Mr. Muhammad, but over the years I have met many like him."

"What do you mean?"

"Muhammad Ibn Baqarah is one of the *shomrim*…," he was interrupted from his explanation when Muhammad returned from the store.

"Yusuf will close up for the night," he informed them. Enoch stood up and walked towards Muhammad and whispering together the men walked away leaving Selah to his thoughts. Selah looked around the apartment and saw the memories displayed on the walls—pictures of babies walking, first days of school, graduation—and felt a pang of envy. He had never known that, and he never would, he was sure. His life was never meant to be ordinary. What a blessing being ordinary seemed to him. In school, he would listen to the other kids complain about their parents. They would bemoan the restrictions, curfews, and rules. Selah would have traded anything to be able to have those same complaints. How much simpler it must be to blend in, to get lost in the crowd. He was never able to blend in. He always stood apart from everyone.

When Selah stood up to see where the men went, they returned to the table. Amatul brought out the dishes, signaling to everyone that it was time to eat. The meal was delicious. Selah spent the time between bites trying to make out any familiar words as the two men spoke to each other in Arabic, both looking serious. After dinner, Selah and Enoch were led to a large guest room, where they would spend the night. At the door, Muhammad turned, looked at Selah, and said, "Goodnight and rest well."

Selah looked around the room. It was clean with two full-size beds, a small dresser with a single candle on it, and an empty bookshelf. Figuring he had been patient enough, Selah asked, "What is a *shomrim*?" Remembering that *shomer* or *shamar* meant to guard, Selah asked, "What are they guarding?"

"The *shomrim* are the guardians of the old ways. They keep the old traditions alive and pass that knowledge from generation to generation. They have existed since antiquity to protect the Word and the Way," Enoch answered as he sat on the bed across from Selah.

"Where are they located? How many—" Selah stopped short when Enoch raised his hands. He stood up and walked to the light switch and turned it off. Plunging the room into darkness, he then walked back to the dresser and whispered *"asha"* to the candle. Selah sat up straighter as a sliver of smoke slowly rose from the wick, and a flame burst from it; the candle was brightly lighting the room.

"Some of man's work pleases me more than others. I prefer this kind of lighting," Enoch said, pointing to the candle, "over this one," and he pointed to the light fixture on the ceiling. Selah sat transfixed looking at the candle, not believing what he had just seen, trying to make sense of it.

Seeing the boy's enraptured face, Enoch realized how much he had to teach him. "How did—how did you do that?" whispered Selah.

"I wanted the fire to light the candle, so I called it."

"You called it, how? You just called fire? I don't understand." Enoch took a moment to consider his answer, then coming to some kind of agreement with himself, he sat down and began.

"After the creation of man's perceivable realm, all things were given a name, a true name. When you know that word, you can command the thing." Looking at the boy, he continued, "The names of all things hold not only their command but their title and their authority. I wanted the fire to light the candle, so I called it."

"*Asha*," said Selah.

Enoch nodded then said, "In the beginning was the word. You must learn the names of things, titles, then you can command them. Solomon has taught you well, it will make it easier."

"Why me? What is happening? I need to understand." Enoch nodded his head, realizing that Selah required at least some explanation before he could rest. The Man of God, the Scribe of the Sages, proceeded to reveal to the *naar* the source of the true name of things and the *Lishon Ha- Qodesh*.

After he finished, Selah didn't know where to begin. His mind was running in all directions.
"What—"

But Enoch cut him off, "Enough. It is now time for sleep; the mind needs rest. We will have plenty of time to teach you once we reach Tsion."

"Where are we going in the morning?"

"We must travel to the gate back to Tsion. It will be a hard journey. Our path is written."

"I won't be able to sleep at all, but I can lay down I guess." With that, he lay down on the bed closest to the window. A few minutes later, Selah missed the smile on Enoch's face when he heard the boy snore. He also didn't see the older man quietly leave the room.

It was still dark outside when the sound of men's voices woke him up. Selah was surprised to realize how soundly he slept. After being in foster care for a few months, he had developed the skill of being a very light sleeper. The world can be cruel to orphans. Sometimes that cruelty is delivered by hands that were supposed to nurture. Selah had heard stories from other children who had been in the system before him about how they were abused and mistreated. Those stories kept him up at night, constantly afraid that he would become a victim as well. Shaking his head at his own foolishness, Selah went to the restroom and quickly got ready for the day. He wasn't sure what it would bring, but he was excited to find out.

The three men were still talking when he walked into the living room. They stopped when he entered the room.

"Good morning, umm ... is it morning? It's still dark outside."

"Good morning, *Habibi*," Muhammad said with a smile.

"Morning, Mr. Muhammad, Yusuf."

"It's good to see you again Selah," replied Yusuf. Selah had met Yusuf a few days after he started hanging out in the store with Muhammad. He was Muhammad's sister's son and had died shortly after Yusuf was born. Yusuf's father was a weak man, prone to vices, and soon after the death of his wife left his young son in his uncle's care. Muhammad considered Yusuf a blessing, and Yusuf considered his uncle his entire life. There is nothing he would not do for him. Theirs was a strong bond of mutual respect and admiration— a son without a father, and a man without a son.

"We will leave soon after you have eaten," informed Enoch. At the mention of food, Amatul appeared to gesture for Selah to follow her to the dining room. There, he was once again treated to a delicious meal accompanied by his hostess's shy smiles. Amatul had no regrets about having four daughters, but she loved the enthusiasm with which the young man ate the food. She considered it a compliment.

After breakfast, Selah followed the sound of the men and went downstairs to the back of the store, where the three men were examining a dark-colored van. Yusuf brought their bags from the room as well as other food items from the store.

"It's still dark outside. Are we leaving?" asked Selah.

"Yes. Muhammad has been most generous with providing us with provisions for the road, as well as transportation," replied Enoch.

"Can you even drive?" Selah said with a chuckle.

"I can do all things through my Maker," replied Enoch with a mysterious smile.

Yusuf called out to review with him once again how to work the gear shift. Yusuf understood that providing for this man was his uncle's responsibility, but it was his uncle's only delivery van, and it hurt to let it go. His uncle had worked hard to provide for his family. Yusuf knew Muhammad would find a way to get another van, but he was human enough to be worried; he lacked his uncle's faith. Understanding that the source of Yusuf's anxiety came from his loyalty to his uncle and family, Enoch obediently listened to the younger man's instructions. One is never too old to learn, or too young to teach.

At the rear of the van, Muhammad walked up to Selah and hesitantly said, "Selah, for each man, when he is in the womb, Allah commands an angel to write four things in his book: his provisions, his age when he dies, his deeds, and whether he will be one of wretched, or one of the blessed. Your deeds, your journey is written. And what is written for you is far greater than my understanding, and beyond my station. Only remember this: You were chosen for a reason, do not let doubt or fear get in the way. Gain wisdom, and with wisdom get understanding. Be strong."

"Thanks Mr. Muhammad, I—" the friends were interrupted when Enoch's shout came from the front of the van— "We're ready." Muhammad grabbed Selah in a hug that caught him off guard. Muhammad didn't realize how fond he had become of Selah. He would miss him, but he knew it was not for him to question the will of his Master.

Getting out of the van, Enoch walked to his host. The two men bowed their heads, embraced, and once again performed the intricate hand gestures. Then Selah and Enoch walked towards the car with Selah on the passenger side. Once he was seated, he looked to see Enoch hesitate at the driver's side door. With the door still open, Enoch said to Muhammad, "By Him in whose hands my soul is, I will protect your friend." This seemed to provide much comfort to the man who was saddened to say goodbye to his young friend. With a final goodbye shouted from the window, the travelers left their hosts.

After a few minutes on the road, Selah asked again, "Where are we going? I asked but you never actually gave a fixed destination."

"We are going to the Mapimi Biosphere in Durango in Mexico."

"Wait, Mexico, we are going to Mexico, yes!" Selah made an excited sound. Enoch chuckled.

This had been the first display of childish delight from the young man, which is why Enoch said, "We have to make one stop first." without telling him where they had to go. He wanted Selah to relax for a while longer. He would explain to him when they got closer to their destination.

Once they were on the road, Enoch became quiet, concentrating on his thoughts. Being an only child and having been in foster care for the past five years, Selah had learned to keep to his own thoughts. So, he was not offended by Enoch's silence; in fact, he appreciated it. It gave him time to process all that he had learned last night. He hadn't asked many questions; the truth is he didn't know what questions to ask, but he knew the things Enoch revealed were true. Selah wasn't sure why, but he knew it was all true. Within the confines of the car and his thoughts, Selah replayed Enoch's revelation from last night.

Enoch had said, "While man was first in the Creator's thoughts, he was last in his creation. Long before your world was created, other worlds were created. And your Adam was also not the first man to be created. There is only one way to begin a story. In the beginning…

The cosmos was created with the first utterance, the first sound that reverberated in the Darkness. From that sound's vibration the cosmos became. Then the Master of the Universe, the Most Merciful and Most Gracious, The Most High and Exalted, Master of the Worlds, created this perceivable world for man with sounds, words, and with numbers. With these words He created all things. Those words and sounds became the *Lishon Ha- Qodesh*, the language of creation. There are other worlds in this infinite universe and the first creations were not of this world but worlds that are not perceivable by human eyes. These worlds were populated by other races of beings, what the humans of antiquity called the *elim* or gods, the *malakim* or angels, and other names, some of which are lost in time. And the Creator knew their true names, for He is the Master of the Worlds.

You see, all of what you call magic is from the *Lishon*. Each act of magic is attached to a special word or true name of a thing. But it is not simply what it is called, it is much more than that. The name bears also the authority of the King or Prince assigned to that thing. The word '*shem*' which means 'name' also means 'authority.' There are other beings, who lord over other things in creation, and are all subject to the Law. The word '*dabar*' means to 'speak' and it also means a 'thing,' because the word is the thing and the thing is the word. *Abara Ki Dabar*—I will create as I speak.

The *Lishon* is made of sound, so it must be uttered, spoken out loud. The non-verbal use of the *Lishon* is dangerous for man. Because man's mind is weak, if he thought of the word 'water' and only wanted a small spring, and then his mind drifts and he starts thinking of someone who has offended him, he could drown the person by accident. The *Lishon* cannot be used for falsehoods, so the Laws are written in it, and any vow or covenant made using it cannot be broken, that is the Law.

Your Adam was created from the *adamah*, the brown of the ground becoming the brown of his skin. Adam was given his name because he was given authority over all things on the *Adama*, the ground from which he came. There were other people created in different parts of the earth, but the one called Adam was singled out to be what Muhammad's Holy Qur'an calls the *Khalifa*, or the successor, inheritor of the race of the gods, the old race, those who were here before the creation of man's perceivable world. He was the chosen one, created in the image of the Elohim to have dominion on not only this world's creation, but also on the unseen worlds and forces that affect this world. Adam was supposed to execute the Creator's will in this world and teach mankind.

It is recorded in the Books that The Exalted One instructed Adam on the true names of all things, the seen and the unseen. He taught him the language of creation, the *Lishon Ha-Qodesh*, The Holy Tongue. He taught Adam the name of all things created in this realm. Then Adam told the gods and angels their names as it was told to him by the Creator. They all accepted his dominion over them, all except one—Iblis. To every rule there is an exception. For Iblis wasn't like the others, he was created to oppose Adam, his adversary. And oppose him he did. For you cannot know good without evil, light without darkness, and cannot earn grace if you never fall. Though one cannot lie using the *Lishon*, there are clever ones who can use it to trick. They can say one thing out loud but mean something else in their minds. Iblis is one of the first Princes and is quite clever.

Unfortunately, Adam had knowledge but not wisdom. He eventually fell from the state of enlightenment when he devised other uses for the knowledge, uses that went against the instructions he was given. His learning brought him to the Whisperer who taught him that which went against the Laws, and Adam fell. The further he went, the less he was able to perceive that which the eyes of man cannot see, he lost dominion over the unseen, he forgot the *Lishon*. When Adam fell, man lost his way in this world. Mankind stopped living in accordance with the Laws, they stopped living within the Laws. They aged, became prey to the animals they once ruled, fell ill, started wars, created their own laws. And as man changed so did the earth. The air became diseased, anomalies grew in man's bodies and on the earth.

But the Creator is Most Merciful and Most Gracious. He sent one from the old race to instruct Adam. He provided him with a book, the *Sefer Ha-Sefarim*, The Book of Books, which contains the names of all of creation. The Book of Books also contains instructions for the one who can read it. One descended directly from the line of Adam is always called upon to be the messenger for mankind, to be the one to read the instructions, return balance, and stop the destruction of this world. You, Selah, are a direct descendant from the one recorded in the Book as your Adam. If one of the Beni Adam knows the true name of creation, he will return sovereignty of this realm to man and not he will be able to rule the unseen. You were chosen to read the *Sefer Ha-Sefarim*, to call creation by name and save this world. You must learn the true names of the gods, and once again gain dominion over them and the forces bent on destroying this world. Once we get to Tsion, I will instruct you on the *Lishon* and the Laws. You must find the *Sefer* and read it. I am no longer of this world and have no dominion outside of that which knowledge of the Laws allows me. I can call things by name and affect other things but only by the grace afforded me in accordance with my station. I am subject to the Law. What I can do in this world is limited, but I can and will protect   you,   this   I   vow."

Chapter Three

Selah was still thinking about all that Enoch had revealed the previous night, when he was startled by his name being called.

"Sorry," Selah said, "I was thinking about everything."

"I know it is a lot for you to take in, and as much as I want to give you time, there is not much time until we reach our destination," Enoch informed him.

Selah looked out the window trying to make out any signs or landmarks to determine where they were. "Where are we?" he asked, becoming concerned by Enoch's tone.

"We are on the island. Selah, I need you to listen to me. Remember when I told you that there are offices, principalities, princes, and kings who reign over certain things?"

At Selah's nod, Enoch continued. "Good. That is where we are going. I wish this was not necessary, but it is. This journey will take a few days, which means three daybreaks. I cannot take the chance of being on the road for days as it leaves us open to danger. By now she will know we are on the way, but it cannot be helped. No matter what happens, let me do the talking, and stay close to me. Do you understand? Never leave my side." Enoch kept looking at Selah until he was assured that Selah had understood the gravity of the situation.

"Who? Who will know about us?" Selah asked, his voice trembling.

The young man was frightened now, very frightened, and Enoch hated the necessity of fear, but it was required to keep Selah alive. The car made a left turn, and in the dark, the only thing Selah could make out was the large shape of some kind of structure or building. There were no lights, and the road was not paved. Selah was impressed by Enoch's ability to maneuver the vehicle in the pitch dark. It was so dark, in fact, that he didn't see the gate until the van stopped in front of it. A disembodied voice told them to drive through. The gate didn't make any sound, but there was a shift in the air, a strange feeling of heaviness, the darkness was denser and once they went past the gate, it became heavier, it felt alive. And it carried with it an instinctive, all-encompassing fear.

Enoch drove an additional mile before slowing down the car. A large mansion could now be seen due to its well-lit entryway. The lawn surrounding it was well-manicured and there were statues of winged creatures at the entrance. If not for the almost paralyzing fear he was experiencing, Selah would have thought the place beautiful.

"Remember, stay close to me, and don't speak." Enoch gave Selah a final warning before opening the door to step out of the car. He stood beside the door, then gestured for Selah to do the same.

As Selah stepped out of the car, the front door of the mansion opened, and a woman walked out. No, not walked. She slithered out of the house. Every step, gesture, even the casual flipping of her hair over her shoulder, was pure seduction. Selah had never seen anyone this beautiful. She had dark alabaster skin—skin so dark she was almost one with the darkness itself. Her long shiny dreadlocks caressed the back of her thighs with each swing of her hips. Selah didn't realize how hypnotized he was by her until she spoke.

"Enoch the Scribe. Well, well, well."

Enoch took a look to the east to gauge the coming of daybreak. It appeared the sunrise was still a few minutes away. With resignation and determination, he walked towards the woman with Selah following in his wake. When he was a few steps away from the van, he placed himself directly in front of Selah, blocking her view. Falaqah smiled mockingly—she wasn't fooled by the Scribe's attempt to protect his charge.

Enoch startled Selah when he said in a loud voice, "As it is written: I seek refuge with the Master of Daybreak, from the evil of that which He created, from the evil of the darkness when it spreads, and from the evil of knotted spells. I am a traveler and seek safe passage, I invoke the name of the one we both call Master."

The smile slowly fell off Falaqah's face and she replied with a sneer, "As it is written: He alone do we worship; He alone do we implore for help." Looking at Enoch with the disdain of someone spoiling for a fight but who was denied that opportunity, she said, "I heard you were no fun, Scribe, but I was hoping for a little excitement. I do hate being denied what I want. But the Law is the Law—you will have safe passage."

Selah saw Enoch's shoulders tense up, which only fueled the raging inferno that was his fear. Seeing his error too late, he began, "Falaqah—" but she interrupted him.
"The boy, however, did not invoke Al Falaq, nor did you include him in your petition."

Enoch backed up and moved closer to Selah. "This is against the Laws. He is under my protection and you agreed—"

She sneered. "I agreed to grant you passage, I kept the Laws. When you invoked Al Falaq, you should have been more careful with your words."

Enoch had been gone too long from the world of man and had not considered the old god's affinity to trickery. A costly mistake, he thought. "Selah, get back into the car," he whispered, but it was too late. From the shadows, forms started to take shape. The shadows moved across the yard and surrounded the van. Running was no longer an option. Backing up until he was touching the van, Selah saw Enoch extend his right arm and whisper "*Chereb.*" A long sword immediately appeared in his right hand, and he crouched low, prepared to fight. As the shadowed figures moved closer,

Enoch whispered, *"seraph"* to his sword. As flames consumed the sword, fear consumed Selah.

Selah was very familiar with fear. It had been a frequent companion when he was younger. Three years after being placed in his grandfather's care, Selah was still withdrawn, prone to night terrors and far too quiet for a seven-year-old boy. Solomon had been concerned about his grandson; he had known too much grief at a very young age. It hurt Solomon so much to see everything the child had gone through. He was an old man and knew that he could forestall death but only for so long. Sooner rather than later, he too would leave Selah. His grandson would be left alone in the world. This, more than anything else, kept the old man up at night. Because of it, Solomon went out of his way to make his grandson happy. And walking on the boardwalk in Coney Island made the child happy.

On a bright sunny day, the two of them would go for a walk on the beach. After a couple of hours collecting shells and running on the sand, Selah wanted some ice-cream. They started walking to the nearest ice-cream shop to purchase the treat. Neither Solomon nor Selah could explain how they got separated, but while walking, they got jostled and Selah lost grip of his grandfather's hands. It was only for a few minutes, but by the time Solomon found him, Selah was huddled in the corner shaking. "I thought you were gone, and I was alone. I was alone again, Grandpa. I was alone." Solomon could not get the child to stop shaking, so they left and went home, where Solomon knew Selah would feel safer.

When he had gone to check on Selah later that night, he was still awake. "I was so scared, Grandpa. I don't want to be alone, it's scary."

"I know you get scared, Selah. Your teachers tell me how anxious you are in school. Losing your mom, that was a hard thing for someone so young. But I want you to know a secret…"

The young boy perked up at the notion of knowing a secret. "What?"

"You are never alone. You see, Selah, Hashem hedges the righteous from all around. He appoints angels to watch over you from the right and the left, front and back. When you are scared, all you have to do is call them and they will appear to protect you. But you have to use your words of power," Solomon had told his grandson.

"Words of power? What's that?"

"They are words that you empower with your faith and your will," Solomon had replied.

"Like a spell?" shouted the boy, excited.

"Yes! Just like a spell," confirmed Solomon.

Selah frowned and said, "But, I don't have any."

"You can make it up, remember, you are the one who gives the words power with your faith and your will."

That night in his bed, the young boy thought all night about his words of power.

A few days later, Selah ran into his grandfather's room shouting excitedly, "I got it, I got it."

"What is it?" asked Solomon.

"My words of power for when I am very scared so my angels can come to protect me."

"Well, now, let's hear it," said Solomon.

With his face set in lines of determination, the young Selah took his paper in his hands and recited his prayer. Moved beyond words, Solomon held the boy in his arms, asking heaven to protect him from harm.

"We will call it *Selah's Prayer*," he said, praying that Selah would never really need it.

Huddled between Enoch and the van, Selah was once again filled with terror. As more shadowed figures formed in the yard, he knew that Enoch would not be able to protect him alone. The old scars hidden inside him resurfaced. He was once again a scared four-year-old trapped in an overturned SUV with his dead mother; he was once again a ten-year-old coming home from school to find his deceased grandfather. He remembered Solomon's teachings, his stories on words of power: "*You are never alone. You see, Selah, Hashem hedges the righteous from all around. He appoints angels to watch over you. When you are scared, all you have to do is call them.*" They will protect you, that's what his grandfather said. Selah knew that Enoch would die protecting him, that this stranger would fight to his last breath to save him.

His grandfather had told him that he had power through faith and will. So in the darkness, somewhere between night and daybreak, trapped between the Scribe and an old van, Selah found his voice and gave power to his words. Slowly standing up, he incanted:

> *There's an angel on my right,*
> *To take away my fright.*

He immediately felt a shift of energy over his head, and a shiver went down his spine. He continued, his voice becoming stronger with each word:

> *There's an angel on my left,*
> *To save me from death.*
> *There's an angel at my back,*
> *To protect me from attack.*
> *There's an angel at my sight,*
> *To serve as my light.*
> *And an angel right above,*
> *To cover me with love.*

From his left a sliver of light grew and shifted into the shape of a man. The same to his right, behind him, and finally in front of him next to Enoch. Enoch never took his eyes off the shades surrounding him and Selah though he acknowledged the new arrivals with a bow of reverence.

The tallest being, who was on Selah's left, addressed Falaqah, "All Beings in the Shamayim and the Earth, all submit to the Most High, the Most Exalted, the Creator, and He alone. They all submit and so do their shadows in the morning and the night. All are subject to Law."

His voice made Selah tremble, until his limbs were shaking so violently that he could barely stand. Soon, he could no longer remain vertical, the floor swiftly came up to meet him, and he lay sprawled on the ground on all fours trying not to pass out. He sensed a swift wind over him, and what felt like feathers brushed his head as something heavy covered him. All around him was the sound of battle—the sound of metal clashing against metal, the sound of pain, the smell of smoke and death. He huddled on the ground under the heavy protective wings, consumed with more fear than he could have ever imagined. The battle raged on as he tried valiantly to crawl into the earth from which his ancestors were formed. Finally, the sounds ebbed and with a final scream of rage, it ended.

Selah lifted his head when a warm hand touched his shoulder. Sitting up, he jerked back when he saw it was one of the beings who had appeared. "Easy, my friend. Do not be afraid," the being said gently. Selah immediately calmed down and felt strength come back to his limbs at the being's touch. With the exception of the one standing with a burning sword at Falaqah's neck, the others and Enoch were tightly surrounding Selah while watching the interaction between the last two combatants.

Falaqah stood frozen with the sword of the seraphim at her neck. "Mikha-El." She sneered, still holding on to her sword. She dropped her sword and bowed down before one of the First Princes, though she did it begrudgingly. She quickly scanned the yard only to observe the small slivers of smoke vanishing into the air as the last remaining shadows disintegrated.

Mikha-El was standing before Falaqah and commanded her, "Leave this place, Dawn is approaching, bringing the Light of Day." Confirming his words, sunlight slowly crept across the front yard of the mansion. With each inch across the yards, the darkness receded.

In defiance, Falaqah said, "You can't stop what is coming, not this time. What are you defending Mikha-El? These talking apes? These beasts of the fields? These are not the people of the Book! They are a lost generation, a depraved horde of disbelievers. They believe in nothing! Their Holy Trinity is money, fame, and vanity. Their altars are social media and television. How can they raise their heads to heaven when it is bowed over their phones? I was more than happy to kneel before them, but they have fallen. The People of the Book are gone!" She stood before him and shouted, "Their children were sold to the four corners of this world and are long lost! They will never return, and their *Khalifa* doesn't have the Book. This world should be ours!"

Turning and walking towards the entrance of the mansion, she said in parting, "I was there at daybreak, the morning your soldiers guided Lot out of that cursed city. We rained down fire and retribution and laid it to waste. I will be there on the day of requital to see man burn."

Mikha-El replied, "Today is not that day."

With one last seething look, Falaqah disappeared inside the mansion.

Addressing the group, Mikha-El looked at Selah. "Was he harmed?" he asked. The question was answered by the one kneeling on Selah's right. "Hannah-El returned his strength, he will be alright." Looking directly at Selah, he smiled. Selah found it difficult to look directly at the beings crowding him. When they made eye contact, he felt light-headed and weak, he could feel the world spinning on its axis, so he concentrated on looking at his chest. Seeing the boy's move, Uzzi-El's smile widened. He understood that the boy didn't yet have the capacity nor the understanding with which to look at him.

"Get him ready to travel. They need to leave as soon as possible." With each syllable, Selah felt his insides tremble with fear. He could not comprehend the sensations he felt around these men. Mikha-El embraced Enoch and they exchanged the intricate hand signals in the same manner as Enoch had done with Muhammad, except the gestures were different. This time, it was Enoch who bowed when the handshake was completed. With one final look at the group, he simply gazed up at the sky and vanished.

A heavy silence descended on the group after he departed. Selah was at a loss for words, trying to get a hold of the thoughts galloping through his mind. A quiet knowledge was creeping into his consciousness, a suspicion was building, one that he needed to address with Enoch.

"He really knows how to make an exit," said the being next to Selah, with laughter in his voice. Selah shook his head at the incredible situation he had found himself in.

"Who are you? What are your names?" Selah inquired of him.

"We are the ones assigned to walk with you," he answered. "We have been with you since you came into this world. I am Uzzi-El." As he spoke, the other beings walked up to Selah and each in turn introduced themselves.

"I am Uri-Yah," the one standing directly in front of him said with a small bow.

"I am Hannah-El. Don't be afraid *naar*," said the one on his left.

"And I am Shamar-Yah."

Selah kept his gaze on the beings' chests, since he still felt faint when he tried to look directly at their faces.

"It will become easier with time," stated Uzzi-El. "As you gain understanding, the gaze will not have that strong an effect on you." Turning to address Enoch he said, "You must leave this place; you have a long journey ahead of you. You will need to seek Nasi, hopefully he will be more welcoming."

"Falaqah was not created to quietly obey. But yes, I will seek him. I cannot spend this much time in the world of man without his blessing," replied Enoch, looking less than pleased by the prospect. This confrontation with Falaqah had opened his eyes. Times were changing indeed. He needed to get Selah to safety quickly. He was proud of the boy. Though he knew Selah wouldn't think so, he had done well this dawn, he had done very well indeed.

"How do you feel?" he asked Selah. At Selah's nod he continued. "We need to get back on the road, we have a lot of ground to cover before nightfall. The night will bring its own problems." When Enoch took a step towards the driver side of the van, Selah exclaimed, "That's it? We just get back on the road? Don't you think we need to talk about what just happened?"

"We will talk, Selah. When it is safe, when we are in Tsion."

"She and her shadow army just tried to kill me! Do you understand? Why? Why me?" Selah's voice broke with the last words. Despite their need for haste, Enoch stopped to address the boy, knowing he wasn't simply asking about the assassination attempt. Seeing the tears in his eyes, Enoch understood that it might have been the only time that Selah had allowed himself to cry. "Selah." He touched Selah's shoulder, but Selah jerked away from his touch.

He shouted, "No!" "Why me? What did I ever do? What crime did I commit? I have lost everything! My mother, grandfather, everything! Now you show up and say I am special, that I was chosen. Special how? Was I especially chosen to be the universe's whipping boy! I am nobody!"

Then his voice turned into a whisper as tears clogged his throat, "I am nobody... I was found in the trash. My own mother didn't want me. I have no father, no name ... I am nobody."

He finally let the tears fall—tears brought on by fear, by a pain so great that he had never spoken of it, not even to his grandfather.

"Selah," Enoch began, but this time he was interrupted by Hannah-El. "You are not 'nobody'. I was beside you while you lay in the refuse bin. In fact, I led her to that one, because it was the safest."

Shamar-Yah continued, "I covered you when the car slid in the ravine to make sure you came to no harm."

Uri-Yah added, "And I lit the way for the driver to find you."

Uzzi-El added, "I have kept you strong, way past your own strength. And we guarded your door in every home you were placed, keeping the monsters away. No, my young friend, you are not 'nobody'."

Enoch finally said, "Selah, in his lifetime in this realm, a man will have three names. The true name given by the Creator, which he will not know until he is standing naked in front of the Lord of the Worlds to account for his deeds. The one given to him by his mother, which will carry all her hopes for him. And the one he makes for himself through his own actions. He has no control over the first two ... but the last one ... the last one is completely up to him. You are Selah Ben Solomon, that is what your mother called you. You have the choice, the power, to make a name for yourself. In your young hands is the future of all creation. There is nothing fair about your life, or the circumstances you find yourself in, but steel is forged in fire. You are stronger than you know ... and I believe in you. At this point, you can no longer go back to the life you once knew, you can only go forward ... in faith."

Feeling strangely rested and tired from the tears, Selah wiped his eyes. "I want to be the man my grandfather wanted me to be. If that man is your chosen one, then I am willing to learn to walk in faith."

Nodding his head in understanding, Enoch once again walked to the driver's side of the car, and climbed in, waiting for Selah to join him. Selah turned to his guardians and asked, "Are you coming?"

Uzzi-El replied, "We are always with you." They all mimicked Mikha-El's gesture—looked up to the sky and vanished.

"Who was that woman? Why did she attack us?" Selah asked once they were back on the main road after leaving Falaqah's mansion.

"Falaqah is the Mistress of the Dawn. She rules the hours before the sun rises. We needed her protection, her consent to travel through daybreak while we travel. Not all the Unseen are fond of mankind. There are those who want man to be destroyed so they can take over this realm.

"My grandfather was one of the *shomrim*, wasn't he?" The suspicion had been growing in his mind. His grandfather's teachings no longer seemed simple or random.

Enoch gave Selah a searching look, not sure if he was ready for this conversation after his recent emotional breakdown. But he answered him anyway. "Yes. Solomon Ben Obed was a *shomer*. He kept the path to the old ways."

"Why didn't he tell me?"

Enoch heard the hurt in Selah's voice. "He didn't tell you because of one of man's greatest fallacies: One always thinks there will be time—time to say the things that need to be said, time to forgive, time to love. But it is written that 'man is like a breath; his days are like a passing shadow.' Selah, if Solomon loved anything in his lifetime on this earth, it was you and your mother. He trusted you, he simply didn't want to add to your burden."

"Did he know what I was?" asked the young man, hurt still lingering in his voice.

"He knew you were set apart, but he didn't know what for. A man's path can only be revealed to him, and no one else."

The two fell into companionable silence as Enoch drove them back to the city. Selah lost in his thoughts only emerged once when they stopped for food. His long silences would usually unnerve people, but Enoch didn't seem to mind. The Scribe, as Falaqah called him, seemed to be a man who also preferred silence over nonsensical speech.

Finishing up his sandwich, Selah noticed they were driving in one of the richest Manhattan neighborhoods. This was a neighborhood with old money. The people were so rich that God sought after them for a loan. These people had power. The people who lived in this neighborhood were the power brokers, the rule makers. Selah has never had any reason to come to a neighborhood like this.

"Where are we going now? Referring to his guardians he asked, "Should I call them?"

"You have already invoked them. They will stay behind the veil, but they are watching. If you were in trouble, they would have already appeared. They no longer need you to make them manifest."

"That's reassuring," said Selah, not wanting another scene like the one at the mansion that morning. "Why are we here? Who lives here?"

Enoch was silent as he maneuvered the van into a parking space. If he had any doubts about what Enoch had just told him, the fact that they were able to procure a parking space made Selah a believer. It was really near impossible to locate a free parking space in Manhattan. Once the vehicle was safely parked at the curb, Enoch turned off the van and turned to Selah.

"We are here to see Nasi, his office is over the Whisperers. Those who whisper in the ears of man, They seduce man into doing all kinds of atrocities. While they have no effect on me, there are plenty of humans between here and Mexico. Without his protection, his whisperers can cause a lot of trouble for us. If I can avoid taking a life, I will do so. Let me do the talking."

Selah and Enoch got out of the van and made their way across the street to stand in front of an opulent Brownstone. Selah blew a low whistle when they stood in front of the Manhattan mansion.

"This is the closest I will ever come to this kind of money," Selah said in awe.

Shaking his head at the boy, Enoch opened the gate and walked up the steps to ring the bell. Selah thought *Even the bell sounded rich.*

A man of indeterminable age opened the door, ushered the duo into the waiting area, and left. Presumably, to summon his master. Selah felt like a tourist in Times Square as he craned his neck and turned around in a full circle while looking at the ceiling. The artist had depicted the entire first book of the Bible, showing the creation and the fall of man. It showed the serpent, but in this scene, he looked as lost and lonely as Adam when he was banished from Paradise.

"Do you enjoy art, young man?" Selah was so captured by the lofty display, that he didn't immediately notice the man walking down the long winding staircase. He was a tall stately man with broad shoulders, dark hair that reached his shoulders in waves, and powerful emerald-green eyes. Selah wondered if any of the people were ugly. From what he had seen, these were the most frighteningly beautiful creatures in all of creation.

Enoch had felt Nasi even before he emerged. Once he reached the lower landing, Enoch addressed him, "As it is written: We seek refuge in the Master of Mankind. The King of Mankind. From the evil of the sneaking Whisperer, who whispers in the hearts of mankind, of the Djinn, and of mankind. We are travelers seeking safe passage. I invoke the name of the one we both call Master."

Nasi answered, "As it is written: He alone do we worship. He alone do we implore for help. Your petition is granted, Scribe, but unnecessary. No harm will come to you or the boy, at least not from human hands." Seeing the look on Enoch's face, he explained, "I was created to entice men, to charge them, to accuse them. I can hardly do that if they no longer exist in this realm. I will cease to have a purpose. They are my purpose, my muse. They continue to provide me with such material that I tell you, I am never bored. Their capacity and creativity for iniquity is absolutely delish. I barely have to whisper. In any case, a painter can't paint without his brushes. They are my brushes, and I can't have them burned to a crisp. You and your charge were always safe from me, Scribe. My existence depends on man."

Enoch nodded, then touching Selah's arm indicated that it was time to leave. Nasi stopped them when they reached the door. "A word of advice, Scribe. There are many who no longer want to remain in this realm and are more than ready to see man take his final curtain call. I have been whispering in human ears since they were etched from clay. They are stiff-necked people. And you will have extreme opposition from my kind. A warrior may be more suitable for this task than a ... scribe."

Reaching for the door handle and stepping out, Enoch said, "Haven't you heard, Nasi ... the pen is mightier than the sword?"

Chapter Four

Once they were back on their way out of the city, the two travelers both resorted to silence as they lost themselves in their own thoughts. It has been almost 24 hours since they had met and already they had developed a routine. Their behaviors synchronized as though they had been traveling together for years. Selah trusted Enoch in a way he had never trusted anyone other than his grandfather. He could no more explain his affinity to the Scribe than he could explain his own acceptance of his situation. But he did, he believed Enoch and he believed *in* Enoch. He didn't feel alone or lost anymore. He didn't know where he was going and he didn't know what would happen when he got there, but he knew with the certainty of the tides that he was on the right path.

He had spent years feeling separate from everyone, different, apart. For the exception of Solomon, he had felt people didn't quite know what to make of him. He always felt that this world, his world, wasn't solid; it felt like a masquerade. He had waited for someone to finally remove the masks to reveal the truth. This was it. The truth was finally being revealed. He was scared but determined to see it through. He wanted to know, to see, to finally understand the feeling of disconnect he carried all his life. This world of magic, kings, and Unseen beings felt more real than the one where he had resided all his life. For that feeling of connection, he was already grateful, and he realized he didn't want to go back.

With that in mind, he turned to his traveling companion and asked, "The night at Mr. Muhammad's house, you lit the candle with one word, *asha*. But with the shadows, you set your sword on fire using a different word. *Seraph*. Why? What's the difference?"

"Intent," stated Enoch. "At Muhammad's I wanted the light of the fire, so I called the fire, knowing it would light the candle. With the *Tselelim,* the shadows, I wanted them to burn, so I called the fire for a different purpose."

"*Seraph* ... burn," repeated Selah with a glimmer of understanding. "But, why use fire?" he inquired of his teacher.

Looking at his charge, Enoch answered, "Because you fight fire with fire. Had one of the Shadows, the *Tselelim*, touched you, your soul would have burned."

"Christ!" whispered Selah, not sure what was meant by his soul burning but understanding that it would have been a fate worse than death.

Having no words of comfort for his charge, for there can be no comfort in the truth, Enoch once more resorted to silence. Selah also joined his companion in silence as he considered the new information that he had received from his mentor.

Enoch weighed his options and thought about what he could tell the boy so close to nightfall. He wanted him sharp and prepared for what was still to come. Night journeys were filled with revelations and dangers. He wanted Selah ready for what was coming next, but he also understood Selah's need to make sense of this new world filled with strangers and stranger things.

Sighing, Enoch explained, "That night, at Muhammad's, I revealed to you that there are other beings who have been created—the unseen. The Most High, Maker of Heaven and Earth, made beings of light and beings of fire prior to making Adam and mankind. Those things, the shadows, were created by fire, and must return to it. As man was made of dirt, they must return to it. That fire dwells in the deep from whence the shadows came. Darkness covers it, and Iblis, one of the first princes, is appointed to rule the Darkness. If you ..."

"The devil, the fallen angel, who rebelled against God, and fell from heaven," Selah added. Everyone had heard this story as children.

Enoch patiently asked, as all sages prefer to teach using questions rather than answers, "If angels were created without free will, and as such follow the commands of the Most High, how then could an angel 'rebel' against Him?"

Selah had no answer to the question, and asked his own. "Then he was created from fire?"

"No. He was created of light as well, for light is as darkness, and darkness is as light to the Most High. In the beginning when the Creator uttered, 'Let there be Light,' He brought forth the light which was perceivable to man, the form of light that can be seen by the human eye. Light that can't be detected by the human eye is what you call Darkness. And it is written that: 'Darkness was over the face of the deep.' The deep is where the fire dwells. It is the home of those who will come forth on the Day of Requital. Iblis is the prince set over to rule the darkness, but even he bows before the Most High and must obey the Laws. The Most High is the creator of all things, and all things work for His purpose," Enoch explained.

Enoch continued his explanation of the use of the different words. "There is the Law of polarity in the universe. Everything has its pole and can be affected by the things that are on the same pole. Happiness and sadness are on the same pole; they are both emotions. You stop being sad by focusing on what makes you happy."

"The same Law applies in all creation. As above, so below. The *Tselelim* and the *seraphim* are made of fire. To stop the *Tselelim* you use the flame of the *seraphim.* Both are fire, but the source is different and so serves a different purpose. The source of the Seraphim's fire is light, and the source of the *Tselelim* is darkness. One is for good, one evil. There can't be good without evil, this is a universal Law. It is the same for the beings made of light and those made of darkness. They are both on the same pole. They are separated only by degrees, just as man is separated one from the other by degrees of ascension. There are good men, men who are righteous and honorable, whose thoughts are pure. There are also men who are evil and whose thoughts are destruction."

He paused his explanations, not wanting to get into a long lesson. They would have plenty of time once they reached their destination. "Selah, as you grow you will learn, and as you learn you will understand. Let it rest for now," Enoch suggested.

Selah realized how much he had to learn and wondered if he had the capacity for it all. How could he, a simple orphan, a widow's son, and the grandson of a simple teacher, a boy with no home, no money, no resources—how could he be the one chosen to serve as the *Khalifa* of this world, when he didn't know anything. Feeling himself becoming overwhelmed, he decided to take his mentor's advice and let it rest for now.

He tried not to think too hard about all that had transpired since they had left Mr. Muhammad's house. Obviously, there would be no rest for him, not yet. From the look of concentration on Enoch's face, he knew that what was coming next would not be easy, not by a long shot. Daybreak had been quite eventful to say the least, and as he looked out the window, he realized that night was falling, and darkness was fast approaching. The previous topic of conversation now seemed a foreshadow of this night. Selah squared his shoulders and braced himself to face the night.

Enoch announced they would be pulling off at the next rest stop to stretch their legs and discuss the next part of their journey. Once they exited the Jersey Turnpike, they drove for several miles until they found a rest stop. Enoch appeared to be searching for a particular space for them to rest. By the time he had located the one he was looking for, the sky was darkening, announcing the coming of the night.

Enoch and Selah left the van to purchase more refreshments and make use of the facilities. Selah found it amusing that even during such fantastic times, the mundane activities of the body were still necessary—they still had to eat, sleep, and relieve themselves. After eating, they sat in companionable silence as Enoch decided what he could reveal to his charge without stepping outside his boundaries.

There was nothing he could do, Selah had to go have his *Mahalak Ba-Laila,* his Night Journey, alone. He could however prepare him, and so, determined, he turned to his charge, but Selah beat him to the punch when he asked, "Was Yahshua your charge? Did you initiate him?" Solomon had also taught Selah about the New Testament. He had taught him about the Christian messiah, a man unlike any other before him or after.

The question brought back centuries-old pain to Enoch as he remembered the face of his last charge—the boy who would grow up to do wonders, the Master of the ages. He remembered the confusion, strength, courage, and fear of the one who would give the world its greatest gift—hope.

"Yes," Enoch whispered. The one word, a painful revelation, dragged through his chest bringing forth grief that was made stronger as he looked into the eyes of the young man who stood on the same crossroad. "He was the last initiate. I have not walked amongst men since he left this realm."

"Was he ever afraid?" Selah asked. "Did he ever doubt his ability to carry out his mission?"

"Yes," Enoch whispered in reverence. "He was far greater than any master before him and after him. And he was afraid, but his faith was always stronger than his fear."

"In life, Selah, there will be days when you will not understand the purpose of it all. This is where faith comes in. Remember that nothing is hidden from The Exalted One. You cannot deceive Him. He will examine your heart and the truth will be revealed. If your faith is lacking that too will be revealed."

"Walk by faith, not by sight, right?"

"That's right," replied Enoch. He would have to have faith—faith in Selah, faith that Solomon had taught him enough to help him get through the next few hours. There were journeys that a man had to take alone, roads that were meant only for his feet and no one else. Selah would have his *Mahalak Ba-Laila*, and Enoch had to have faith that the boy would prevail.

Selah rubbed his temples for the fifth time since they had returned to the van. What started as a throb was fast becoming a pounding. "Are you alright?" inquired Enoch.

"Yes, I just have a headache. It came out of nowhere. That is strange." From one minute to the next, the pounding had become an all-out migraine, with light sensitivity and nausea. Selah began squinting his eyes and breathing heavily to help squelch the nausea.

Observing his discomfort, Enoch suggested he lie down in the first seating row of the van. He walked around the vehicle, pulled the door open, and waited while Selah moved to his makeshift bed. The pain was so bad that Selah didn't actually believe he could rest, but he was willing to try anything to relieve the pressure in his head.

He fell asleep the minute he became horizontal.

At the front of the van, Enoch's head bowed in submission. He gave praise, "Glorified be He Who carried His servant by night from the Inviolable Place of Worship to the far distant place of worship, whose precincts we have blessed in order to show him our signs. He and only He is the Hearer, the Seer. *Ameen.*"

When Selah woke up and opened his eyes, he was startled to find himself lying down on the ground looking into nothing. He couldn't see anything for miles. No trees, roads, buildings, nothing, just an empty valley. It didn't look like anything one would expect to see on the East Coast. The last thing he remembered was the pain in his head, and Enoch mumbling something he couldn't make out. "Maybe, I am dreaming," he said out loud, though it didn't feel like a dream, even for someone who had very vivid dreams. If not a dream, then what was it?

Recalling the past encounters, Selah became concerned that this could turn violent. "Enoch! Enoch!" he cried without any response. He didn't actually expect one, so he resorted to plan B.

"There is an angel on my right ..."

"There is no need for fear." The response came out of nowhere. Selah abruptly turned, tripped on his feet and found himself on the ground looking up at a very tall man, masked by shadows.

"Your guardians cannot assist you, not here, not now," said the shadow man.

"Who are you? You will tell me your name," Selah commanded as he stumbled to his feet. He couldn't see the man's face since most of his features were obscured in the umbra of some unseen object. The moon's light was casting shadows all around the man, when he moved around, his face remained unseen, always blocked by the shadow, similarly to someone who wore a mask made of shadows. He was tall and of a muscular build. As he walked around Selah, his movements were graceful and powerful. Selah felt he was being weighed and measured.

The man took his time answering the questions. "The stars were called to witness. I am Ha-Tariq, the Night Visitor, He who knocks at the door, the Morning Star."

"The what? Where am I?" demanded Selah.

"You are in *Ha-Maqom*, the Place. It is a crossroads of sorts for travelers. Where you go from here depends on your journey, and what is written in your book," replied the Visitor.

"Are you like a guide or something? Am I supposed to pass some sort of initiation? Why do you come at night? Do ..."

"A knock at the door in the night is jolting. It alarms, frightens, always grabs attention. A person cannot deny hearing a knock at the door when it comes at night," he answered.

"I don't know what you mean," stated Selah. "Where is Enoch, I am his charge, I …"

"Fear not. No lasting physical harm will come to you here." Ha-Tariq looked up. Selah followed suit and drew his breath in a loud gasp. Never had he seen a night sky such as this. The firmament was lit up with stars. With colors so beautiful, it brought tears to his eyes. No human hand could ever create such wonder of colors and light. *My grandfather would have loved this* thought Selah. Solomon used to love looking up at the sky. He once took Selah on a stargazing trip to Big Pine Key in Florida. At the time, Selah had thought he could see Heaven, but that memory paled in the face of this glorious display. Selah watched as stars shot across the sky like lightning going back and forth.

He was startled when Ha-Tariq asked, "Do you comprehend what the Morning Star is?" Selah shook his head and shrugged.

"The Morning Stars were present at the creation of your realm and were given a human soul to watch over. Your father, the Father of the People, Abraham, was promised that his descendants will be as numerous as the stars in the sky." Ha-Tariq returned his gaze to the heavens and continued, "There is no human soul which doesn't have over it a watcher to mark his days and inscribe his deeds in his book. When a man stands before his Maker, on the Day of Requital, he will be given this book, and by his deeds will he be judged. We record the deeds of man and, therefore, we are present when he is being tested."

"Am—I—dead?" stammered Selah.

"No," he kindly replied. "I would not be the one to lead you on that journey. This is a different trial to determine the course of your life, Ben Adam. You are Ben Adam, son of the People, and as such are given the gift of rebirth." He continued, "This night is your *Mahalak Ba-Laila*, your Night Journey, when you will be weighed, and where you will choose your path to stay entrenched in the worries of man and a man's life or to become more. You may choose to be the sheep or to become the shepherd. A man cannot serve two Masters or live in two worlds. He must choose one of his own free will, that is the Law."

Ha-Tariq turned and there stood a lone tree, old with gnarled branches reaching up in supplication. Tied to the lowest branch was a donkey. Ha-Tariq freed the donkey from its bindings and walked it over to Selah. "This is Buraq, she will assist you on your journey." From the satchel thrown over its back, he removed a vial and poured oil from it over Selah's head, while mumbling a prayer under his breath. Selah felt the soft caress of the oil as it poured over his head till his chin, and then the collar of his shirt. It comforted him for reasons he did not understand.

"You must choose one of these paths." Ha-Tariq pointed behind Selah, and in the same empty space from a few minutes ago, now lay six different paths, each leading to different directions forming a large circle around them. "Once you can no longer see the tree in your wake, you will begin to encounter others who will examine you, but they cannot come near this place."

Looking at the paths diverging all around them, Selah inquired of his shadowed guide, "Which one am I supposed to choose? What am I supposed to do?"

"Only you can decide which way to go. Each path has infinite possibilities. Infinite possibilities for good and infinite possibilities for evil. The devices of a man's heart will choose his path," stated the shrouded man. Selah made a slow circle as he considered his options. How would he choose? He didn't like the "infinite possibility for evil" part of the spiel. He stopped, closed his eyes, and took a deep breath. Once again, he thought of his grandfather and searched his brain for the lessons or stories his grandfather taught him. He now understood that the stories and teachings were not random. As a *shomrim*, Solomon knew that this day would come, he knew that Selah would need the teachings. If ever there was a time for them, this was it. He stood there indecisive for a few minutes, then a memory suddenly came to him.

On the weekends, Solomon enjoyed taking Selah on adventures, when they would pick a new place or neighborhood to visit. They visited parks, zoos, museums all over the city, not just in Brooklyn, but also in the other boroughs. They tried different cuisines, as long as they met Solomon's food restrictions. On one such occasion, the duo got lost in Manhattan. Not being familiar with the city, Solomon stood contemplating which road would lead them back to their train. Suddenly, the old man shrugged and started walking. Being a curious child, Selah asked him how he determined which way to go. "East," replied Solomon, "Travel ever eastward my son."

Opening his eyes, Selah asked, "Which way is the east?" Ha-Tariq pointed to the road right in front of Selah. "May the words of your mouth and the meditations of your heart be acceptable. *Shalom Aleicha.*" Then like a flash of lightning he disappeared leaving Selah standing in the clearing with Buraq.

Selah stood in the clearing for a few minutes looking at Buraq. "I guess it's just you and me. Can you talk?" After a few seconds of no response, Selah sheepishly said, "Well, duh, of course you can't talk, you're a donkey." And chided himself for letting his imagination run away with him. But then again, he reminded himself that the past few hours had been beyond anything his mind could have ever conjured up.

He grabbed the satchel and looked inside. Nothing. *Why give me an empty bag?* He thought. Then dismissed it, thinking this was the least of his worries. Feeling neglected,

Buraq nudged her companion, neighed and moved her head, appearing to say, "Let's go already."

"Alright, alright, we're going," replied Selah, no longer having any good reason to procrastinate. He grabbed the end of Buraq's leather rope and started walking eastward.

They walked for hours with Selah periodically turning to check if the tree could still be seen. And it could. He started to feel that maybe he had been the butt of some cosmic joke, maybe the tree was keeping pace with them. "That would be really messed up if your master was playing me," Selah told Buraq. The donkey shook her head. Selah abruptly stopped, looking at the animal in amazement. "Can you understand me?" Again, the donkey nodded her head in affirmation. "I am Dr. Doolittle!" exclaimed Selah with a laugh. Amused by the donkey that could communicate, Selah picked up the pace with his companion.

After some time, Selah noticed that they were now walking at an incline. Turning to check on the tree, he realized it was no longer stalking them. There was also a shift in the air, and his ears started to hurt the way it did when there was a change in altitude. Once they cleared the incline, Selah and Buraq stopped looking at the scene in front of them.

There, in the middle of the valley, was a banquet table laden with a smorgasbord of delectable foods—fruits, meats, every kind of dessert to delight a glutton's heart. Across from them, on the other side of the table, stood a man, tall, very tall, with an austere but not unkind demeanor. As they drew closer, Selah started to feel that pull, that inescapable weakness of his limbs. The way he felt around the Beings who defended him at Falaqah's mansion. Even Buraq started to become agitated. When they were just a few feet from the table and the man, Buraq stopped and kneeled.

"*Shalom Aleicha*," mumbled Selah, kneeling before the being. He didn't really have a choice; his legs refused to support him. His heart was pounding and he felt light-headed, week-limbed, and afraid.

"Selah Ben Solomon," called the man.

"Here I am," replied Selah.

"Rise and be strengthened," commanded the man.

Selah rose to his feet. His trembling had stopped and he felt stronger, though he still could not make eye contact with the Being. He stood waiting for instructions on what he was supposed to do next. Buraq remained kneeling, her face to the ground in complete submission.

The man pointed towards the table. "In his lifetime a man will make choices. They may seem mundane, but in fact, they determine the kind of man he is." He continued pointing at the table, which was now empty save for three goblets.

Selah walked closer to the table to examine the goblets. They were made of copper. One goblet contained wine, another water, and the last one milk. Frowning in confusion, directed a question to the man's chest. "What am I supposed to do?"

"Choose," he replied. "Choose a cup. The wine, the water, or the milk, then drink it."

Selah stood before the cups, not knowing which one to choose. He thought that perhaps it was one of those tests where the simplest answer was the correct one and started to reach for the water. He hesitated. It didn't feel right, so he pulled back his hands. He considered what each substance meant. Wine was used for celebration. Wine was also a sign of wealth. He thought of those auctions on TV, where a bottle of vintage wine cost thousands of dollars. He had no need for wine—this one was an easy decision. He then considered the water. Water was life—nothing could grow without it. It also purified everything. On this journey with holy beings shouldn't he want to be purified. He started to reach for the water and, for the second time, stopped. He looked at the cup of milk. That's the one he wanted. Milk meant nourishment, a mother's love, home, sustenance. He was a child and doesn't a child feed on milk? A child is given milk until he is weaned from his mother and is able to eat solid foods. He was humble enough to realize that he was only a child. What did he know of anything? With humility, he chose the milk. He lifted the cup to his lips and drank it. It tasted sweet, like it was laced with honey.

The man bowed his head in acknowledgement, then said, "An infant needs milk until he is weaned from his mother."

Selah knew he had made the right choice.

Hidden in his memory came the words from one of the psalms of Ascent: "As a weaned child am I in my mind." He wasn't weaned yet though, he had much to learn. Understanding the lesson, he recited, "My heart is not proud, I do not aspire to great things or to what is beyond me."

The man bowed in acknowledgment, then he disappeared in the same manner as Ha-Tariq, in a flash of lightning. Buraq stood up from her reclining position and nudged Selah, indicating that they should move on. The man, the table, and all it contained vanished leaving only the cup in Selah's hand as a token of their visit. Selah put it in the satchel and threw it on Buraq's back. The two travelers continued on their *Mahalak*.

Chapter Five

Buraq was a great traveling companion. Selah realized how helpful she was not long after leaving the clearing. The path was still clear, but due to the darkness and differences in terrain, it could be difficult to walk. Buraq always seemed to know when to walk on the grass and when to return to the path. She helped him avoid ditches, pitfalls, and even a snake. He became very attuned to her moods. Whenever she sensed harm or trouble, she would simply stop walking. It was Selah's cue that something was wrong.

They had been walking in companionable silence for a while, when Buraq abruptly stopped on the path, huffed and shook her head. "What is it? What's wrong," Selah asked, feeling nervous. When your magical donkey's Spidey senses started tingling, an inexperienced traveler had to pay attention.

"*Arach.* Traveler" the word was spoken out of nowhere. Selah jumped; he had never heard a voice that deep in his life. The voice was so deep, he imagined if the darkest pit had a sound, this would be it. On his left, a man emerged, dark and aggressive, dressed in pure black. Selah started to back up, when he felt a hand gently touch his shoulder. On his right, a short, old woman appeared. She was round and grandmotherly with mahogany skin lined by age, and coyly gray hair pulled on top of her head. She was dressed in purple and carried a jar of water in her arms. "Careful, young traveler, stay on the path," she whispered to Selah.

Selah moved closer to Buraq whose attention seemed to be focused on the man. In fact, the animal had moved closer to the woman. Selah decided to trust his friend. He turned his attention to the man who appeared to be a threat.

"Grandmother," greeted the man. The older woman bowed her head in acknowledgement.

"Layil," she said in reply, acknowledging his greeting. "Still walking around scaring children in the dark, I see."

He laughed. His laughter was as dark and deep as his voice. "I have come to bear witness, as I am entitled. I am the night; he travels under my jurisdiction," he said, his voice heavy with contempt.

"You have drawn your veil; you have introduced yourself, so your job here is done. Leave the *arach* to his travels; he is protected on his path," she reminded him, her voice strong with authority. The disparity between them was absurd. The tiny old woman bent with age facing the man who was coiled like a predator stalking his prey. But she wasn't afraid, in fact, she looked ready, she wanted him to test her mettle.

The man was silent for a beat, then bowed mockingly. "I only meant to meet the *naar* and warn him of the dangers of traveling at night."

"The only danger he faces tonight is from the likes of you and your ilk. You have given him your warning. Leave this place." The last part was a command, plain and simple.

Selah released a breath when the man vanished. "Thank you," he said to the old woman. She moved closer to him and gently touched his cheeks. "I am Saba," she told him.

"Thank you, Saba," he repeated.

"You are welcome, my own. There are laws that bind us, but the old ones can be very tricky. Where is your cup?" she asked him.

Selah opened the bag that was tied on Buraq's back, removed the cup, and handed it to her. She took the cup from him, filled it with water and ordered him, "Drink all of it. It will help you see the truth of things." Selah did as commanded. When he was done, he showed her the empty cup.

She nodded her head in satisfaction. "Good. He will not bother you again, not tonight. He will remain hidden until the time when hidden things are revealed. Stay on the path and trust Buraq. She will help you avoid the obstacles. Lean on her when the road gets steep, so you don't lose your footing. Do not speak to anyone else on the journey."

"Don't talk to strangers, I got it." Selah smiled then pointed out, "Aren't you a stranger?"

"I am no stranger to you. We are connected. You feel the bond between us?" Selah nodded his head, because it was true. He did feel a bond with the woman, so much so that he wanted her to draw him in her arms and comfort him. Maybe she could read his mind, because she did just that. When she pulled away from the warm embrace, she kissed his forehead and blessed him. "Blessed be your coming and your going. Blessed will you be in the field and blessed will you be in the city. This is my blessing."

As a parting advice, Saba reminded him, "Stay on the path, mind Buraq, she will not steer you wrong. Safe travels, my own." Then she too disappeared. Selah felt a strange sense of grief when she left. Buraq nipped his shoulder to get his attention.

"Ouch! That hurt, you know," Selah admonished her. He placed the cup back in the satchel and placed it on Buraq's back. Taking a fortifying breath, he asked Buraq, "You ready?" The donkey nodded her head in response to his question.

Selah took hold of Buraq's rope, winding it around his hand for a tighter hold. He was also walking closer to the animal, feeling a sense of security from her close proximity as they continued on their journey.

Soon the path became almost impossible to navigate. They started the journey in a valley, where the terrain was flat. There were ditches to avoid, but it had been manageable. Now, they were climbing on the side of a mountain. The further they went up, the harder it became for Selah to maintain his footing and he found himself slipping with every step. When they made a particularly rough turn, Selah lost his footing and started flailing his limbs but was unable to stop his momentum. He went over the ledge.

His body hit the side of the mountain. Hard. Very hard. He felt his shoulder pull; the pain was excruciating. He almost let go of the rope that tethered him to Buraq. The only reason he was able to hold on was because he had tied it around his hand. Looking up, he could make out Buraq's shape as the donkey neighed in concern.

"I'm okay!" he shouted. Slowly, he ascended back up the side of the mountain as Buraq backed from the ledge, pulling her young friend back to safety. Once he crested over the ledge, Selah laid on the ground, panting. "Yeah, let's not do that again." Buraq neighed in agreement. Climbing to his feet, holding his shoulder, he faced the donkey, touched his forehead to hers and said, "Thank you, my friend." Buraq rubbed her head against his shoulder in comfort, then nudged him forward, indicating that they needed to move on.

"I know, just give me a minute," replied Selah to her silent request. Once his heart stopped galloping in his chest, Selah took a moment to do a quick triage on his body. His shoulder hurt a lot, but he was able to move his fingers, so he assumed it wasn't dislocated. His ribs and arm were also sore, but again nothing he couldn't deal with later. *What the hell kind of dream is this, where pain actually hurts!* He thought a person was not supposed to feel physical pain in a dream. Selah once again wrapped the leather rope around his hand, this time he chose the other hand. He also moved towards the inside of the mountain. Buraq was preternaturally better equipped at navigating this treacherous terrain. He would let her lead the way.

They walked for hours with Buraq leading the way. She had managed to keep both of them alive until they finally turned a corner of the mountain and found themselves in a large open plain once again. Selah breathed a sigh of relief as he surveyed their new environment. The plain was wide open, with nothing in sight for what seemed like miles. Selah turned to look behind him. The mountain they had climbed was gone. Simply vanished. When he faced forward, he discovered that he and Buraq were no longer alone. In the middle of the plain stood a lone figure, patiently waiting for the pair to approach.

Selah and Buraq walked towards the figure, unsure of what awaited them. When they were just a few feet away from the figure, Selah started feeling that familiar weakness. Once they were close enough to make out its features, Buraq took a knee and would move no further. Unable to hold himself upright, Selah also took an involuntary knee, and fell to the ground.

"Rise and be strengthened," commanded the man.

Selah felt the strength return to his limbs. The pain from his sides was also gone and there was no physical indication that he had taken a nosedive off the side of a mountain. He slowly rose to his feet, prepared for his next task. For a second, he had a fanciful thought: *This is how Hercules must have felt during his trials*. He turned his attention to the being standing before him. "Shalom *Aleicha*," he said to him in greeting.

"*Aleicha Shalom*," the man replied. He extended his arm, guiding Selah's attention to the objects next to him. Embedded into the ground were a sword, a scepter, and a small staff. The sword—a four-feet-tall instrument of death—looked deadly with the sharp blade piercing the ground. It was an object created to mete out justice and judgment. The handle had an intricate carving of a dragon. The scepter was tall and slender. The head was encrusted with jewels of various colors, each one more brilliant than the other; the entire body made of pure gold. Even enthroned in the ground as it was, it was taller than Selah. The wooden staff was about the length of Selah's arm. It was smaller than the other two objects. It was smooth but carried knots throughout its length.

"Choose one: the sword, the scepter, or the staff," ordered the man. "Then take it."

Selah looked at the objects lined up for his inspection. The sword caught his attention first. For a boy who had spent most of his life being afraid, the sword represented power. Power that people like him, disavowed and disenfranchised, were not privy to. What would it feel like to be that strong, powerful, and invincible? Selah was sure that whoever held that sword would be invincible. He thought of the stories he had read about knights and kings. King Arthur and his Excalibur, and King David and his *giborim*, they had been invincible. But in the end, Selah recalled, David didn't build the temple. His son did. Solomon—whose name means "peace"—was the one who brought peace over his kingdom. A man of war was not a man of peace. Selah recalled Ha-Tariq's earlier advice "a man cannot serve two masters." Selah wanted peace, not bloodshed. He wanted to lead, but he didn't want war to be his path.

The scepter was a king's ceremonial staff. It represented the king's authority, power, and sovereignty over his land. Selah recalled Solomon quoting the Miqra. "The scepter shall not depart from Yehudah, nor a lawgiver from between his feet until Shiloh comes. And unto him shall the gathering of the people be."

Solomon felt that it was an indication that the scepter would not stay with Yehuda but would leave once the true ruler came. Solomon had explained that true authority was divinely ordained. Besides, Selah didn't see himself as a king. The scepter, with all its pomp and circumstance, ornaments, and jewels, was not for him.

The staff was also a symbol of leadership, but it was for one who had altruistic authority. If the scepter was a ceremonial staff, then the staff was the scepter of divine authority. Moshe had led his people to freedom and destroyed the Pharaoh's army without ever touching a single person. His staff was the extension of the Creator's hands. Selah reached out his hand, grasped the staff and pulled it out of the ground. He held out the staff, and channeling Enoch said, "It is written: And יהוה said unto Moshe, what is that in thine hand. And He replied, 'a staff'."

The man bowed his head to Selah in acknowledgement. "The staff is used in three ways: to draw the sheep together, to keep them on the right path, and to protect them from themselves," he instructed. "You have chosen the *Mustaqeem*, the right path. It is the most difficult path, the one which encompasses all three. We give our revelations only to those who have knowledge and seek understanding. Ben Adam, we among those who dwell in the heights recognize you by your name and you have been granted the blessing."

Saying that, he was gone, leaving Selah holding the staff. He and Buraq were once again alone in the open valley, the path still clearly defined. Selah could make out a tree line on the horizon. With the staff in his hand, he and Buraq made their way towards the forest in the distance.

The companions stopped just before they could enter the forest. Every tree in the forest was white; leaves, and trunks were as white as the driven snow. Addressing Buraq, Selah said, "Are you ready for this?" Buraq nodded her consent and took the first steps towards the forest. The forest had the strange glow that occurs when it is snowing outside; it smelled of pine—pure and clean. Not too far into the forest, Selah came upon a large structure, which resembled a palace.

The palace walls were made of ivory. No wonder they couldn't see it from outside the forest. The palace had blended seamlessly into the environment. Standing right outside the walls, Selah could not see an entrance. Buraq and he walked around the entire structure, thinking that perhaps the entrance was located somewhere in the back of the building. Nothing.

Returning to the front—Selah could not tell one way or another—the pair stood looking up at the palace. "Do you think we have to climb it? The walls are too smooth, there is nothing for me to grip. What do you say girl, any ideas?" he asked Buraq, but she only stared back at him.

There is no gate, or door for me to open, I cannot climb the walls, Selah thought. *What other way can I enter? Then* it came to him. Walking closer to the wall, Selah knocked on it. There was a tremor as the wall shifted, and slowly cracked open creating an entrance large enough for both of them to enter. Buraq did not hesitate and walked straight through; Selah followed behind his fearless companion. They entered into a large banquet hall with wooden floors and a high arching ceiling. The sound of Buraq's hooves echoed throughout the hall. In the center of the hall stood a lone man.

"*Shalom Aleicha*," greeted Selah.

"*Aleicha Shalom*," returned the man. What stood out to Selah was that everyone he had met on this journey had been of exceptional height. Not this man though. His smooth copper skin shone with health, he wore a blue-and-white robe, had a full beard and intelligent and kind eyes. He appeared to be a man in the prime of his life, mid-to-late forties.

"Welcome to my house. You have entered on your own free will and merit. You have been redeemed." Taking a pouch from his robe's pocket, the man handed it to Selah, instructing him, "When you reach the water, you will be asked who redeems you, tell him 'Yedidiah Ben Dawad redeemed me as first born. My flesh and my heart are circumcised.'"

Selah opened the pouch, stuck his hands in, and pulled out a handful of gold coins. "Thank you," he said to the man.

"This is my blessing," said the man. "May He who grants honor, grant you honor. May He bless you and the works of your hands and make them prosperous."

Selah put the money in the bag, and out of curiosity, he tried to staff as well. The staff immediately vanished inside the bag. Shaking his head, he marveled at the bag, then placed it once again on Buraq's back. Bowing to the man, they turned and walked out of the palace. Once they passed over the threshold, the door sealed itself shut. Then, the house and the forest were both gone.

Buraq walked on, leading them forward. Selah was tired. How could all of this walking be happening in one night? The sun should have come up by now, but judging by the night sky, dawn was nowhere near. They walked on for miles and miles before Selah brought them to a halt. "You hear that?" he asked Buraq.

The donkey nodded. "It sounds like running water." The pair continued on until they could see the shoreline. Living on the east coast, Selah has seen the ocean on many occasions. However, this ocean was breathtaking. The water glittered like diamonds in the moonlight. "Wow," Selah mumbled. There were no words to describe the wonder lying before him.

At the shore, stood two figures. One was standing inside a small boat, and the other on the sand next to it. Selah's heart seized when he saw the man standing next to the boat. "Grandpa!" he shouted and ran at full speed towards his grandfather. He collided into Solomon, clutching him with all the strength in his young body. He didn't realize that he was crying until Solomon's rough fingers wiped his face. The old man pulled back from the child of his heart, searching his face. Smiling, he wiped Selah's tear-streaked face. "What's this? Come now, none of this," said the old man.

"Grandpa. It's really you! I miss you so much." Crying, Selah could barely get the words out. His heart was so full, it was overflowing in tears. "You will never believe the past couple of days." The two fell into their old routine with the old man patiently listening as Selah recounted his adventures. When he was done, Solomon stated, "I am so proud of you. You have done well, but this is only the beginning."

"Do you remember what I told you about the root of the word 'Hebrew'?" he asked his grandson.

"You said the word Hebrew or *ibri* comes from the word '*eber*' which means 'to cross over'," answered Selah.

"That's right. This is an *eber*, a crossing." He turned to show Selah the water. "You must cross the *Mayim Chaim,* the water of life, in order for you to be born again. Do you understand?" At Selah's nod he continued, "We can't tarry any longer." He pulled Selah closer to the boat. "Once you cross over, you will be forever changed, as it is written." The man named Solomon, during his human journey, tried to lead his soul's earthly tether—the one person that kept him attached to the human world—to the ferryman.

"Wait grandpa. I don't want to leave yet. I want to stay with you longer. There is so much to tell you. You have been gone for so long." The boy clutched his parent's shirt. He wasn't ready to let go, not yet.

"You must let me go," whispered his grandfather.

"Please don't ask me to do that," sobbed Selah.

Solomon wrapped his only surviving child in his arms. "Ah, Selah!" he sighed, as the child continued to weep. "Do you know why I named you Selah?" he asked, pulling his grandson back so he could see his face. Selah shook his head.

"Selah means to lift up and exalt. In a psalm, it is the break in the song where the psalmist would lift up his voice higher. But the other word 'Sala' also means to weigh something. In the Torah, that is when the reader is supposed to meditate on the word he had received. When you were placed in my arms, I knew this was my moment, my purpose, my way to exalt the Most High. Everything that I did after that moment was for you. My purpose was fulfilled when you came into my world. I took the moment to weigh, measure, and examine my life. And when I crossed over, there was no lack found in me, because I loved you. I had fulfilled my life's purpose. Now it is time for you to fulfill yours, and by doing so, you will continue to fulfill mine. I am not gone, Selah, as you live and breathe, so do I," stated Solomon.

Selah held on to Solomon's arms, the very arms that had become frail towards the end of his earthly life. But now his grandfather's grip was as strong as his voice. He recalled all the moments in his life when Solomon's teachings guided him, not just tonight, but on various other occasions. He thought about Enoch waiting somewhere for him to return, and he thought about his responsibility—the Book, the *Sefer Ha-Sefarim*.

He wasn't sure how or where he was supposed to find this Book. However, he knew he had to find it, and learn what he must in order to stop beings like Falaqah and the others who wanted man to be destroyed. There was a purpose, a grand design to his life. He wanted to discover it. He let go of his grandfather's sleeve and wiped his final tears.

Solomon kissed his grandson's forehead, then said, "Heaven bless you and keep you in all your ways. That is my blessing. Now, you must leave." Taking the boy by the arm, he pulled him to the boat.

The man on the boat had remained silent during this entire exchange. When they reached the boat, he finally asked, "Who redeems you?"

Selah turned to Solomon and said, "I will see you again. I will make you proud, I promise."

Solomon replied, "I am already proud."

"Who redeems you?" the man asked again.

Selah replied, "Yedidiah Ben Dawad redeemed me as first born. My flesh and my heart are circumcised."

The man reached out his hand. Confused, Selah looked at his grandfather for an explanation. "The gold," said Solomon. Going over to Buraq, who had been patiently waiting, Selah took the bag and withdrew the pouch of gold, giving it to the ferryman. As soon as the man took it, a ladder tumbled out of the boat. Selah hugged his grandfather, thanked him for his teachings, and walked over to Buraq. "I don't suppose you can come with me?"

Buraq shook her head. She nudged him towards the boat. The boy wrapped his arms around the donkey and said, "Thank you." Selah climbed into the boat. From the stern of the boat, Selah watched his grandfather and Buraq fade from view. He stood looking into the distance long after the shoreline disappeared. He was leaving behind his thoughts on the past. His attention was brought to the present when the boat came to a sudden stop. Selah could not see anything for miles. He asked the ferryman, "Is this it, is this where I get off?"

The ferryman informed Selah, "Ben Adam, the hour of your death has been recorded. You may have the answer to one of three questions. You may know how you die, where you die, or when you die. Which will it be?

Selah looked out onto the water; it was like looking into eternity. The horizon is forever out of reach, because once you reach the point you are looking at, it ceases to be the horizon. That was life. The point was not to know but to learn. That is the human experience.

He understood the reason Enoch hadn't told him about this, because he was sure he knew about it. He hadn't told Selah, because there was no way to prepare someone for certain experiences. How do you prepare yourself to fall in love, deal with heartbreak and betrayal? Knowing will cheapen the experience in some way. Faith. That's what Enoch wanted him to understand. Faith was moving forward without knowing what was coming, it was a steadfast belief that whatever happens is meant to be and has a purpose.

He answered the ferryman, "I don't wish to know any of it. I choose to do this blindly." Smiling, he said, "I would rather walk by faith than by sight." The ferryman bowed in acknowledgement of his choice, then pointed to the water. Selah was caught off guard. "Wait, you want me to jump in?" asked Selah. The ferryman nodded his head. Selah walked to the edge of the boat and jumped into the water.

When his body hit the water at first there was a push inside of him, but thereafter nothing. He couldn't feel his body, there was no body, just him. His consciousness floating in the nothing. *I am dead*, Selah thought. There was no fear, only resignation and ... peace. There was no white light, only darkness, consciousness, and peace. Then Selah felt a pull, like he was being pulled through a vacuum. His breath returned first, followed by his awareness of his body when he face-planted on what felt like a rough carpet. He gasped loudly. His heart pounded and eyes hurt from the glare of light, which he quickly recognized as sunlight.

"Breathe, Selah, breathe." It was Enoch's voice. The Scribe was crouched next to him, rubbing his back. He helped him sit straight up on the seat.

Selah felt weak, tired, and hungry. Very, very hungry. The sunlight was hurting his eye. He quickly closed his eyes; he was not ready to open them yet.

"Easy now. It will take a minute for your body to recuperate. You must be starving. I have food and water once you feel able to eat," Enoch said softly. When he was a child, Selah had the flu and was in bed for a week. This was the same feeling of weakness. "Why do I feel this weak? Man, I am hungry!" Selah complained.

"The weakness and hunger you feel are normal. You have been sleeping for a while, give your body time to adjust." Enoch said, rummaging in the front seat. He returned to the back where Selah sat and placed a wrapper in one of his hands and a bottle in the other. Selah drank his fill of water before asking, "How long have I been sleeping?"

There was a pause before Enoch answered. "Three days. You have been sleeping for three days. We will cross the border into Mexico within the next two nights."

Chapter Six

So much had happened since the evening he had first met Enoch. It was only three days since he had discovered this new world. Three days, and now he was awake, or as his grandfather put it, was born again. There was so much to process, his brain was having a hard time keeping everything in order.

It all felt like a dream. Not Enoch's world, that felt real. It was the "waking" world that now felt illusory. He now understood this world to be a reflection, a copy of the real world. There was a small part of him that wished he hadn't fallen into this rabbit hole, but the larger part of him was happy and relieved. There was freedom in being a sane person in an insane world. Maybe it was the other way around.

Thinking about his Night's Journey and remembering his grandfather's message strengthened him. *God, he missed him.* He understood the importance of all he was doing and that one day he would sleep with his fathers and be with his grandfather again. There was a lot of work to be done, and miles to go before he could sleep. He also had a lot of questions.

"During my Journey, I met a few people. Am I allowed to ask about them and the Journey itself?" asked Selah. There were rules to this thing, and he was learning them as he went.

Enoch nodded and said, "You may ask me questions, and I will help you understand. But, remember, each person's journey is different and, as such, they will encounter different people."

"How was I gone for so long? It felt like one night to me."

"Time works differently in different realms. To you it felt like one night. But while your soul or spirit traveled, your body remained here experiencing time as it is in this realm," Enoch explained. Selah nodded his head in understanding. Solomon had once told him that a thousand years on earth was but a day to God.

"Ha-Tariq said he was the Night Visitor, 'The Morning Star,'" Selah continued.

"Ha-Tariq is not a name but rather an office or title. They were present in the creation and are called to witness and initiate the Night Journey. They are the watchers who keep records of man's deeds."

Selah nodded, then asked thoughtfully, "He gave me a donkey as a guide, why a donkey?"

Enoch answered Selah's question with a question of his own. "What is the tenth commandment?"

Selah had to think about it for a minute. "Thou shalt not covet thy neighbor's property?"

Enoch asked, "And which properties are listed? His house, his wife, his servants, his ox or his donkey. You know that what is written is for those with understanding to search out the truth.

You know a 'house' doesn't designate the physical location. The donkey is more than an animal in this realm, rather, it is the one that leads a man on his *Isra*."

"It is telling the initiate not to covet another initiate's path," Selah stated.

"That is correct," Enoch confirmed. "Moshe placed his wife and sons on a donkey to return to Egypt. Abraham saddled a donkey to take Yitzhak to be sacrificed. Abigail rode out to meet Dawad on a donkey. Baalam's donkey stopped him when he saw the angel sent to kill him, and Yahshua rode into Yerushalem on a donkey. Each one of them during their initiation had chosen their own path. It is written: 'A donkey knows its master's manger. Her way is always true.'"

Selah was silent for a while, with his head down as he processed the information. Then he looked up at his teacher and informed him, "I chose the staff."

Enoch nodded. "I suspected that would be your path. You have a humble spirit and a kind heart."

Selah smiled. "You didn't think I would want to rule? To be king?"

"There is authority given by man and authority given by heaven. Regardless of what you chose, you will be given authority to rule. The sword, scepter, or the staff determine the path to your kingdom." He paused to make sure Selah understood what he said.

"Selah, you are here to reclaim the authority of the Beni Adam given to them by Elohim. When you chose the staff, you instinctively chose the path of the chosen people— the one set for the children of those written in the Book. You have chosen the right path. You will one day rule the seen and the Unseen and return balance to this realm. You will need the sword to claim the scepter, and the staff will help you remain true to the Laws and keep your reign righteous."

Selah saw the truth in what Enoch said regarding his chosen path, but now he was gaining faith in himself and his destiny. He thought about the others he had met on his Journey. He remembered the ones who had frightened him and those he had instinctively trusted. "I met an older lady, her name was Saba," he said smiling.

Enoch returned the smile. "Ah, Grandmother visited with you. She is called by many names: Wisdom, Chokhma, Nana Buruku, Kokyanwuhti. She is the mother of the chosen people. She will teach you and guide you. It is a great blessing that she chose to speak with you," Enoch said.

"She defended me, protected me, I think from the one named Layil," said Selah.

"Protection was not needed; Layil could not have harmed you. Not physically. He could have frightened you, persuaded you to a different course, or made you stray off the path, but he could not have harmed you. That is the Law," clarified Enoch. "Layil brings the veil of night, darkness. It is not him to fear, but those who walk with him. The whisperers, *Ra-ah*, *Rasha*, they are the ones to fear. However, they are no match for Saba. It is written: 'By Wisdom, the earth was founded. She protects her children and holds great power among the Elohim.' Saba wasn't protecting you; she was claiming you and making it known to all." Searching Selah's face, Enoch asked, "Was there anything else?"

"She poured water in my cup and had me drink it," informed Selah.

"Yes. It is called the *Mayim Haim*, the water of life. In her wisdom, she knew the choice you would make. She fortified you," replied Enoch.

"There was also a man inside a white house located in a white forest. He redeemed me by paying for my passage. Who was he?" asked Selah.

"Did the man tell you his name?" asked Enoch.

"Yes," replied Selah. *Yedidiah Ben Dawad, the name means something.* Thought Selah. Enoch waited for his pupil to arrive at the answer by himself. The best teachers help the pupils find the answers rather than giving it to them.

Yedidiah Ben Dawad, Yedidiah son of Dawad, translated. He knew then who it was. Enoch saw comprehension dawn on the boy's expressive face and smiled.

"King Solomon!" exclaimed Selah. "I was redeemed by King Solomon?" Yedidiah was the name God gave Solomon when he was born. The name was delivered through the prophet Nathan. His true name was Yedidiah." Selah looked at Enoch and smiled in awe.

"You found your way to the house in the forest of whiteness. It is the seat of the king and a symbol of his authority. You were chosen as the heir," said Enoch. "Your heart was examined, and you were not found wanting anything. You were guided in the night and redeemed. You were anointed and properly initiated. Your initiation was complete and now the real instructions will begin once we arrive in Tsion."

While they sat in the van talking, Enoch gave Selah time to adjust his system back in this realm. They had miles to cover before reaching their destination. They could no longer linger where they were. Enoch had pulled over to a quiet, deserted farmland. There was nothing but trees and sunshine surrounding them. It was a beautiful place. The boy had gone through an extreme experience and he needed time, but time was the one thing they could not afford right now.

"Selah, we have to move on. Try to get some rest and finish the food. We still have a lot of ground to cover," Enoch told Selah.

Selah nodded, understanding Enoch had given him as much time as he could, but now they had to move on. They were so close to the gate. He could feel it. A pull, a slight buzz in his ears, a sharpening of his senses. Whatever it was, it was close. "I'm ready to go," Selah told Enoch. And he was.

They traveled for several miles, as Selah watched the countryside go by, before he asked Enoch, "Where are we? What is in Mexico? Why do we need to go there?" Selah's question broke the silence ruling inside the vehicle.

"One of the gates to Tsion is there," replied Enoch. His answer brought a look of confusion to Selah's face.

"I don't understand, isn't Zion in Jerusalem or somewhere in the Middle East? I mean that's what I thought."

Enoch gently shook his head. "No. All that is in heaven and on earth belongs to the Most High. His home is in the heights and He reigns everywhere. As I said, there are different paths that a traveler takes to Tsion. Each one leads to a different gate, and different gatekeepers."

"Gatekeepers? Are they like Falaqah and Nasi?"

Shaking his head, Enoch reassured the boy, "The gatekeepers bar the way to Tsion, so that only the righteous may pass." Saying this, he paused. He could see the questions dancing across Selah's face, so he began again.

"There are twelve gates into Tsion, the Holy Mountain. Eight can be found in this realm for the righteous, masters and the sages, as it is written. Another four, called *The Four* or the *Arbot*, can only be reached by those who have ascended to other realms, worlds higher than this, the people who have gone through Aaliyah, the ascension. Those are the gates of the *Yadadim*, the *Mashiachim*, the *Malikim*, and the *Malakim*.

They can travel back and forth to Tsion to worship the Most High. Those who are still corporal can travel through the eight gates, but only those who are pure spirit can travel through one of the *Arbot*. The *Arbot* are located in each corner of the world and are also guarded by gatekeepers.

The eight gates are located throughout the world and can be accessed by those with understanding, by the one who sees not with the eyes. Man relies on the eyes to perceive his universe, the same eyes that can't see in the dark. He is limited in his knowledge and understanding of this world because of it. Your scientists understand that man can only see a small fraction of the light, but what they don't understand is that once upon a time, man had dominion over darkness itself. The lower he descended, the less he could see.

In this world, there are sacred places from which the gates can be accessed during certain months, certain days, and times of the day when they are open. It is written: 'The gates don't open until the heat of the day.' One does not access Tsion in the night, night travel is reserved for higher beings.

It is written: 'Great is יהוה to be exceedingly praised in the city of our God, the mountain of His Holiness. Beautifully elevated is the joy of the whole earth, Mount Tsion. Elohim dwells in the city of יהוה in the Holy Mountain. יהוה loves the gates of Tsion more than all the dwellings of Yaqoob. Glorious things are spoken of Her, the City of Elohim. Ameen.'"

Selah was silent during Enoch's explanation and exaltation. Always one who thought before speaking, he took his time to ruminate on what he was told before finally saying, "You talk of ascension and those who ascended ... Do you mean the ones who have died? How does one ascend?"

"Master Yahshua revealed that in order to see the gates you would have to be born again. The soul must go through its *Isra*, Night Journey, until it reaches the truth and gains understanding of his path. With understanding, it can obtain wisdom," Enoch explained. He searched Selah's face for an indication that he had understood what he had revealed. He couldn't explain too much in their present circumstances.

"Initiates are able to access the gates? How do they know where they are?" Selah asked.

"They discover where it is. The gate through which you enter is determined by the path which you have chosen," answered Enoch.

While contemplating his answer. Selah watched as the verdant countryside became a desert. Realizing Enoch hadn't answered his first question, he asked again, "Where are we?"

"We are in the northeastern parts of Arizona," stated Enoch.

"Arizona? What is in Arizona?" asked Selah.

"We need to pick up something from an old friend. She does everything in her own time. She doesn't get many guests, so she loves company," explained Enoch.

They pulled off the main road and drove for almost an hour before Selah could make out the shape of a structure in the distance. A house was protected in the shade of a towering mountain. It was small and appeared to be made from adobe; the windows and doors were tiny. The roof looked to be also a terrace where a figure stood watching the approaching vehicle.

"Welcome to Hopituskwa, home of the Hopi, the Peaceful people," Enoch said with a gentle smile.

Selah watched as the figure disappeared inside the structure. By the time they pulled in front of the house, the person opened the door. She was a tiny, older, native woman; her silver hair fell over her shoulders in waves. Her small stature made Selah smile. At almost six feet, he knew he would tower over her. Enoch stopped the car and jumped out with more enthusiasm than when he had first met Selah.

"*Lolma*, Kaya," he said while embracing her.

"*Lolma*, my old friend," she said, returning his embrace.

She turned her shrewd gaze to Selah. "*Lolma*, my young friend," she said to the boy with a small, welcoming smile. Addressing both of them, she said, "Come, your journey has been a long one. There is nothing to fear here, not from man nor beast, seen or unseen. This is sacred land and it cannot be crossed; it is perceived only by those who were reborn from the water of life." She then led the weary travelers inside her home.

Enoch nodded his head, reassuring Selah. Selah found himself trusting the words of a stranger once again. But like Saba, he felt a strange connection with Kaya. With faith, Selah followed Enoch into Kaya's home.

The house appeared larger from inside. There was a fireplace in a corner, and an old staircase that led to the second floor. The walls were decorated with landscape paintings. The corner opposite the fireplace held what appeared to be a shrine of some kind. The space was large, and each room was delineated by a different color. The house was warm and inviting. This was the most at ease Selah had felt since leaving Mr. Muhammad's house. There were logs neatly stacked up in a corner near the fireplace which Kaya used to expertly start a fire within seconds. Selah heard her say "*asha*" before the flames lit up the room. Turning, she smiled a secret smile at the young man, when she noticed his look of surprise.

"Dinner should be ready soon. I was expecting you two before sunset," she informed the weary travelers.

"Thank you for your hospitality ma'am," replied Selah.

"Brave, humble, and polite. This is good," Kaya said, addressing Enoch. She walked out of the room towards the back of the house where Selah assumed the kitchen was located. Enoch too walked out of the house, only to quickly return with their bags.

"We will be spending the night here. In the morning, Kaya will lead us to the kiva," Enoch informed Selah.

"What is a kiva?" asked Selah.

"It is a sacred place that holds certain artifacts. We need one of the items in order to open the gate." Their conversation was interrupted when Kaya walked back into the room with her arms laden with dishes. Both of them hurried to relieve her of the items. She instructed them on where to place the various dishes on the table, then the three of them sat down to eat. The food was delicious and filling. Selah didn't know the names of most of the dishes, but he didn't really care. His belly was full, the room was warm, and he was safe. He had no complaints.

After dinner, Selah helped Kaya clear the table. When he offered to help wash the dishes, he quickly found out that she was stronger than she looked—she practically shoved him out of the kitchen. He and Enoch sat quietly on the couch. Neither one felt the need to participate in idle small talk. Selah enjoyed their silences almost as much as their conversations. It was a rare thing to find that person with whom one could sit in silence and still feel comfortable. Once she was done with the kitchen, Kaya came back to her guests. "Come," she told them, handing them each a colorful blanket, and leading them out the back door into the twilight. Out in the yard was a large fire pit around which lingered the smell of smoke, indicating it had been recently used. Near the pit was another neat stack of logs which Kaya used to start a fire. The three of them sat quietly for a while. Selah looked up at the evening sky. The stars were putting on quite a show.

"There has been a lot of chatter among the Kachinas for the past few days. The spirit world is ablaze with talks about you, young man," Kaya told Selah.

"Everyone is picking sides and preparing themselves for the shift. Among those who have not chosen a side, there are some who have lost all faith in man, while others just want to go home. They are the one who will determine the final outcome. Those who reside in this realm will tip the balance." She exhaled a weary breath.

"These mountains and this desert have waited so long for this. The land has been patiently waiting, guarding its treasure and praying for this day to come. My people and I have been waiting for you for generations." Her wise eyes looked at Selah with fondness.

"How long have your people been here?" asked Selah.

"Ah, that is a long tale, for long nights," stated Kaya.

"And one you love to tell." Enoch told her. They both laughed at a private joke, in the manner of old friends reunited.

"Now let's see..." Kaya went on to tell Selah the legend of the Hopi's creation. She told him that before the creation of the earth, there was endless water. Then the Sun God and the Spider Woman created the earth and all it contained. They sang a song, one that had never been heard before, and from that song the earth formed. They then created man from mud to toil the earth and care for the animals. They covered the man with a white cover to give him breath or spirit. They commanded man to obey their words and to call on them if they needed help. They then ascended into the heavens in shining glory.

The crackling of the logs brought Selah out of the trance of her story. There was something magical and sacred in passing down a story from one generation to the next. He found himself enchanted by Kaya's voice and the cadence of the story. The similarities between the Hopi's creation story and that written in the Miqra was not lost on him. Solomon had once told him that all of mankind worshiped the same God, that people just called Him by the name which He revealed to the ancestors. Selah understood the idea of the universal consciousness, the connection between each soul in this world. There wasn't a difference in faith, it was the demonstration that was different.

The three sat quietly until the fire burned down to ashes. Kaya then led them to rooms on the second level. Selah was asleep before his head had even hit the pillow. He didn't hear Enoch and Kaya's conversation in the hallway. Not that it would have made a difference, because they spoke in a language as old as time, which hadn't been heard by man in thousands of years. They spoke in Lishon HaKodesh.

Chapter Seven

The gentle stroke of a hand on his shoulder woke Selah up from his sleep. After the first year in foster care, Selah had stopped sleeping heavily. He had learned there were unseen dangers and predators everywhere. In one of his first placements, the foster father would spend a lot of private time with one of the younger boys. He would take the boy out, just the two of them. The boy would return from their trips together shaken and broken. The child would lay in his bed silent and numb. Selah was terrified the man would turn his attention on him. He was there for a week, before the foster father requested he be removed. Soon after, he heard the man was arrested. Selah had never been able to sleep soundly since then. However, since he met Enoch, his sleep had been the most peaceful since his grandfather's death. He opened his eyes to Kaya's gentle face.

"Time to wake up, love, you must continue your journey," she whispered, "breakfast will be prepared by the time you come downstairs." She left the room as quietly as she had entered it.

Selah smiled. He wasn't sure why he was smiling, but it was probably because of the calm energy, peace, and love in Kaya's house. It was a tangible feeling that could not be denied. With the small smile still on his face, he washed up and met Kaya and Enoch downstairs in the kitchen.

"Good morning," Selah greeted Enoch and Kaya. Enoch was at the table waiting and Kaya was standing at the stove.

"*Nukwang talongva*," replied Kaya, bringing a steaming bowl to the table. She indicated for Selah to sit and placed the bowl in front of him once he was seated. "*Paas-i* it is very hot," she warned him before returning to the stove to get a bowl for Enoch.

The three of them sat at the table and ate their breakfast in companionable silence. The soup was delicious. It was accompanied with sweet cornbread and very strong tea. Selah complimented Kaya on her cooking once he finished his meal. "*Askwali*," replied Kaya, then her expression changed and became more serious. She and Enoch exchanged looks; Enoch nodded in agreement to an unspoken question.

"Selah, you have completed your *Isra*. I know this because you are here. You have chosen a difficult path. One that is challenging for even the strongest among us. Your faith, will, and strength will be challenged constantly. You will have to make choices that will challenge you as a man and will have you question the righteousness of your quest. I cannot help you with these choices or challenges, but I can give you that which has waited for you for thousands of years." Kaya stood and walked over to the couch and retrieved a white cover with intricate designs. She handed it to Selah. It was soft. Selah could not determine the material, only that he had never felt anything this soft.

"*Pew'i*, come." Kaya walked to the back door with Selah and Enoch closely following in her wake.

They walked out the house and stood in the yard facing the mountains. Kaya opened the wooden gate leading them out into the desert. It was still dark outside. The sun hadn't started its circuit across the sky. Selah wrapped the blanket around his shoulders as the air was still very cold in the desert. Kaya led them through the desert, until they reached the bottom of a mesa.

"Many, many years ago, the Sky People fell from the Heavens. They were tall visitors who came from the sky in shining circles. Those Sky People were messengers from Maasaw. They taught my people secret things and a language foreign to all the other tribes. The Sky People then divided our tribe into two clans, one clan, the Hisatsinom were given the Tablet of Destiny. The Hisatsinom then disappeared in order to protect the Tablet. They went into the desert and hid themselves and the Table of Destiny from mankind. My ancestors were given the Staff of the Gods and they have protected the Staff since then. We have maintained a secret kiva away from all the other clans. Only those chosen as guardians of the Old Ways know about this kiva. We have waited many years for this day, waited for you Selah."

She led them to the side of the mesa where a small path could be seen leading up one side. They trekked to the top of the mesa and were confronted by a large mountain. It seemed different from the others, set apart from them. The air smelled and tasted different too. Selah licked his lips to find that the air was sweet. Frowning at the sweetness in the air, he followed Kaya and Enoch, who had been very silent since breakfast, since this part of the journey was Kaya's to lead. Selah decided to keep his observations to himself since neither one of his companions seemed to be disturbed or surprised by the change in climate. They halted once they reached the bottom of the mountain.

"The rest of the way, you must go alone," Enoch informed Selah. This was the first time since they had left the house that he had addressed Selah.

Looking around, Selah shook his head. "I am really getting tired of treacherous-looking mountains," he mumbled. Turning to his guide, he asked, "Let me guess: I am supposed to find this Staff of the Gods?" At Enoch's nod he added, "And you can't tell me anything, because there are rules, and you can't break them, right?" again Enoch nodded. "Of course." Selah resigned to this new adventure. Counting on the temperature rising with the sun, and not wanting to get the beautiful cover dirty, Selah handed it to Kaya.

"No, you must keep it with you. It belongs to your people, Ben Adam," Kaya replied. She had never referred to him by that title before. Selah nodded and wrapped the blanket around his shoulders. Kaya pointed to the side of the mountain, showing him the way up. With a final look at Enoch, Selah started up the mountain.

The temperature changed drastically as he ascended up the mountain. Selah was grateful that Kaya had insisted he keep the blanket. He tied the blanket around his shoulders to keep himself warm. The land was rough, and the ascension was physically taxing and required he use his hands for support along the way. Selah recalled his *Isra*, and his near fall off the mountain, but this time there was no Buraq to help him and falling off this mountain would carry far heavier consequences.

The sun made its ascent, bringing higher temperatures, and the blanket's warmth became a hindrance. Selah considered leaving it on the trail and returning for it on the way down, but in the end decided to tie it around his waist. Climbing alone was daunting, and having the blanket was reassuring. He smiled at the thought of having a security blanket.

The smile fell off his face when the landscape plateaued. The land was flat and dry and in the center was a large circular hole. Selah took a few minutes to search the area and catch his breath. He estimated a few hours had passed since he had started up the mountain. He was tired, hungry, and thirsty, but determined. He cautiously walked to the edge of the drop and looked down into the deep. The air coming out of the kiva was cool, and he could smell sweet cinnamon and honey.

Selah took another look around to see if there was a ladder or rope he could use to descend into the kiva. Nothing. He started a slow walk around the entrance, and on his second pass, he saw a protruding rock about four feet down the mouth of the kiva. Selah had to get on his stomach to see it clearly, but yes, there it was. On closer inspection, he could see that there were additional "steps" leading into the dark space. Selah did not know how far the steps went, or where it led. He stood up and secured the blanket tighter around his waist and he pulled his T-shirt over it, determined to keep it as clean as possible. He then went down on his knees and lowered himself to the first step. Keeping his hand on the wall, he slowly started down into the kiva.

On the third step, some pebbles fell into the void. Selah held his breath waiting to hear when they landed. He heard nothing. Either the kiva floor was soft and plush, or this was the longest staircase in history. Taking a deep breath, the *naar* continued down the stairs. Out of the blue, Selah remembered one of his grandfather's favorite psalms: "From the depths I am calling you Hashem, Hashem hear the sound of my voice. Give an attentive ear to all my supplications." Then Selah added his own supplication, "Please, please be a light for my feet. Amen." The young man continued downwards and downwards. He lost track of time, his ears started to feel pressure from the change in altitude, but he still continued downwards.

He finally stopped his descent when his legs began to shake. Then, before he could correct his footing, he lost it and fell. A scream escaped from his lips before he could pull it back, but it was abruptly silenced when he landed gently on the soft ground. He looked up and could not make out the entrance; in fact, the darkness was so complete that he couldn't even see his own hands. *How am I supposed to find anything when I can't even see my own feet?* he thought. The oppressive darkness was shocking to him. Selah unwrapped the blanket from his waist and opened it to wrap it around his shoulders. As soon as he opened it, the blanket started to glow, spreading light all around. Selah was finally able to see the cavernous space where he stood and an old man patiently sitting in the center of the dome.

The room was circular and from the central point extended into four different rooms or caves. There was a small round hole in the floor of the kiva. Selah returned his focus to the man, waiting for him to acknowledge him.

"Hello," Selah said, and noticing the Native American designs on the blanket around the man's shoulder, he tried again and said, "*Lolma*," in greeting.

"*Lolma*," replied the man and waited.

"Umm. Kaya sent me, she said I would find something here." Selah didn't know what he was allowed to say, so he decided to be circumspect. He waited for a heartbeat, and when he received no answer from the man, he asked, "What is your name?"

"I am Ahote. I am the keeper of this sacred place," the man answered.

And he went quiet again. *Okay*, Selah thought, *this is going to be hard*. He walked over to the man and sat down with his legs crossed. On his right was the small hole. Selah gave it a quick glance but focused on the man. The older man simply looked at him and waited.

"Do you know why I am here?" Selah asked.

"You are the only one who can answer that question," Ahote replied.

Selah considered his next question carefully, having realized that Ahote only answered the questions he was asked. *Ask and it will be given unto you, seek and you shall find*. While he was thinking, he gazed around the room for inspiration. Since the central room led into four additional dark caverns, Selah asked, "What are these caves?"

"When the first people came into this world, they traveled the four worlds. Each cave leads back to the old worlds," Ahote answered.

"Is the sacred item hidden in any of these worlds?" asked Selah.

"Whatever you are searching for always starts with you," advised Ahote.

Selah wasn't sure what that meant. He tried to formulate his next question with Ahote seated across from him. Selah thought about the item itself. Ahote had said, "Whatever you are searching for always starts with you," so the answer was in him. *So, the Staff must already be here, or near her*e, he thought. He once again perused the kiva. Nothing. There was nothing else in the room, other than the two of them.

According to the Miqra, Moshe was given the *Mateh Ha-Elohim*, the Staff of the Gods. There was no burning bush here, or loud voice, only a silent old Native American man. The *Mateh* was given to Moshe to do God's wonders. Selah sat up straighter as he suddenly remembered a conversation he had had with his grandfather long ago.

It had been their last Passover together. Selah had been the one responsible for most of the preparation for their Seder meal that night. Solomon had been weaker then and most of the household chores were left up to Selah. The two of them conspired to hide Solomon's increasing weakness from Ms. Johnson, knowing she would have removed Selah from the home. That night, during dinner, Solomon recounted the tale of the Exodus as tradition dictates. Halfway through the tale, Solomon stopped the story and said to his grandson, "You do realize what the *Mateh* was, don't you?"

Selah shook his head. Solomon explained, "Moshe didn't need the staff to do wonders. The power was given to him as the one chosen for the task. What Moshe lacked at that time was faith. Faith in himself, faith in Hashem. The staff is an extension of Hashem's hand and a connection between Him and Moshe. A link from the world of the Unseen and this one. The power, however, was always inside Moshe, sleeping, waiting for him to awaken."

Seated on the kiva's floor Selah opened his eyes. He didn't realize when he had closed them. Ahote was still sitting in front of him, but he had a smile on his face. It was the smile of a teacher who was proud of his pupil. Selah remembered the staff he had chosen during his *Isra*. It occurred to him that the staff was about the length of his arm, almost like an

104

extension of his arm. Selah pulled the blanket down and exposed his right arm. Slowly, feeling a bit foolish, he raised his arm up with his palm facing upward to receive what he was requesting. All of a sudden, there was a shift in the air and the sweet smell became more pungent. A strong wind blew into the kiva, ruffling their clothes. The strength of the gale pushed Selah forward and he had to use his arms to prevent his face from crashing into the ground. When the wind died down, Selah looked behind him and saw the small hole that was now in the center of the room.

"The *sipapu* has chosen to reveal it to you *Pahana,*" said Ahote who now stood in front of the hole in the center of the cave.

Selah rose from his seat and took the small steps towards the hole. There in the center, illuminated by an ethereal light, was the Staff of the Gods.

Selah reached into the *sipapu*, as Ahote had called it, and removed the Staff. He felt his breath quicken and something beautiful, magical, and powerful moved inside of him. The feeling walked around his soul, then sat firmly. Selah had never experienced such a feeling before and would not be able to define it to anyone. But it was there, the presence, the feeling. It was a consciousness, or awareness perhaps. A presence that was always there in him, but he had never noticed it before. Selah felt humble tears come to his eyes and he turned his head to avoid Ahote's gaze.

"Pahana, you must now return to the world above. Your work is only beginning. We have waited a long time for this moment. You must travel to the world of the Gods. When you return, you will find the Hisatsinom and bring back the Tablet of Destiny and save this world. This is a great day for the Kachinas." Ahote bowed low before Selah.

"Thank you, my friend." Selah returned the low bow. It was time for him to leave. He walked to the rock-hewn steps and started his ascent. Turning one last time to say a final farewell to Ahote, he stopped short—the kiva was empty. Holding the Staff in one hand, Selah placed the other hand on the wall to steady himself and started his way out of the sacred place.

The ascent was just as nerve-racking as the descent. The darkness was not as oppressive thanks to the blanket's glow, but now Selah could see how deep the kiva was and how far he would fall should his steps falter. Slowly, he made his way to the surface until he was able to see a sliver of light. His relieved breath echoed in the void, and he continued walking up the stairs. Once he reached the entrance, Selah hesitated. He needed both hands to pull himself out, but he felt that putting the Staff on the bare ground would be disrespectful. After considering different options, he realized he had no other choice. He placed the Staff over the ledge and grabbed and pulled himself out of the kiva.

Once he was out, Selah lay on the ground on his back, looking up at the moon. His stomach was growling, his leg muscles were aching, and his arms felt heavy, yet, he had never felt more at peace. The soft breeze ruffled his clothes making him aware that he was lying on the blanket. He jumped up and swept his hands over the cloth to clean it—the blanket, too, deserved his respect. The blanket was no longer glowing. Above ground, it looked like an ordinary blanket, nothing special, but down in the kiva, it had become invaluable. At first glance Selah couldn't see its worth. Only with time, discernment, and at the time of need did its worth become evident, and now it was priceless. Selah gently folded the blanket and placed it safely under his clothes. He picked up the Staff and began his journey down the mountain.

He wasn't sure of the time, only that an entire day seemed to have gone by. Or at least he thought it had only been a day. After his *Isra*, he had learned that time was not linear, and worked differently in different places. He was certain, however, that Enoch, Kaya, food and shelter were all waiting for him down the mountain, so on he went.

Selah heard Enoch's and Kaya's voices before he saw them. Once he turned the corner, he was able to make out the shape of the two figures huddled around a small campfire. They saw the young man at the same time. They rose to their feet and waited for him to get closer to the fire. Kaya moved forward with her arms outstretched when she saw Selah with the Staff clutched in his hand. "Pahana," she whispered, her voice breaking with tears, and embraced Selah. From the comfort of her arms, Selah made eye contact with Enoch who nodded his head, a small proud smile on his face.

"Well done," Enoch said.

"Umm Kaya?" Selah inquired, after his third attempt to pull himself out of her arms.

"I am sorry. My people have waited for so long and suffered so much, and now the time is finally near. You are Pahana, you are the one who will bring back the Tablet of Destiny and save my people. You will bring back order to the world. The realm has been on the verge of destruction for so long, but it is finally time." Wiping her eyes, she gathered herself, looking at Selah with hope, joy, and fear in her eyes. It was the fear of being so close to happiness—the most numbing fear of all. But she visibly strengthened herself, squared her shoulders, and said to her companions, "Let us go back to the house; my leg of the journey is at an end but yours is only beginning. Pahana needs sustenance and rest, he will have it."

The old woman resolutely started walking back to the house in the dark, guided by a light unseen to her companions. Selah followed in her wake quietly. Enoch lingered long enough to put out the fire. Kaya was right, their work was only beginning. The more time he spent with the young man, the more Enoch had grown to care for him. This was the hardest part of his calling. Teaching, grooming, and then sending them out into the world to fight in a battle they didn't start, for people who might not even appreciate it.

He didn't know what would happen, but he knew that Selah's life would be filled with light, power, and tragedy. As the Teacher, the Scribe, the Man with the Inkhorn at his side, the one who kept the records, and marked the ones chosen, Enoch would do his best to prepare Selah, and have faith.

He gave the mountain a final longing glance, "*Masha Allah*, God has willed it," he said out loud and followed behind his charge and Kaya. In the morning they would leave this place and continue on to Mexico. It was time to go through the gate.

Showered and seated at the kitchen table with a cup of strong tea, Selah finally asked the question that lingered at the back of his mind. "Why did you call me Pahana?" He was the first to break their peaceful silence. He didn't mind the silence. Before Enoch, silence had indicated a lack, now Selah understood that silence was a great teacher. It taught patience, which was necessary for acquiring knowledge; it made room for understanding, and it led the way to wisdom.

"There is a prophecy among my people. The ancestors warned us of a war that would come. The war will be between the people who first revealed the light in the old world. They will burn the sky and destroy the earth. Many will die and a new reign will begin, one of terror and oppression. Then the *Saquasohuh*, the blue star will shine, and the Pahana will come. Before the Great Spirit hid herself, she gave the Sacred Tablet, the Tablet of Destiny, to the Hisatsinom to guard, and only when Pahana returned, will he be able to locate the Tablet. He will unite the Staff with the Tablet, and usher in the fifth and final world, the world for the peaceful, the humble, the meek, and the righteous. This world today is *Koyaanisqatsi*, it is a world out of balance, out of alignment and order," Kaya explained while she walked around the table and placed plates steaming with food.

"This realm is already preparing itself for the new era. New seeds, new stars, and new species are being discovered by the scientists. Across this earth, spiritual beings are awakening. They feel the shift in consciousness. They are searching, waiting for the fifth world," she continued, sitting at the head of the table to join her friends for the meal.

"You think I am this *Pahana*?" asked Selah, holding his spoon to his mouth.

"I know you are, for the *sipapu* would only reveal the Staff to Pahana, no one else. The Tablet has great power, and so does the Staff. My people have guarded the Staff for generations. We were chosen because the Hopi are peaceful people, because we do not seek that which is greater than ourselves. You were given the Staff which will lead you to the Tablet." Saying this she started eating, signaling the end of the conversation.

Selah didn't need additional encouragement to dig into his plate; he was famished. It turned out that he had only been in the kiva for an entire day and it was approaching midnight. He would not usually eat this late, but circumstances being what they were, he was learning to be flexible. The three friends ate in companionable silence. The food was warm and delicious. Selah felt that Kaya's cooking was unparalleled. Solomon had taught him to appreciate different cultures, and that training, along with the esoteric ones, had been advantageous to him.

As they finished their meal, each of them processed their own thoughts and prepared themselves for what was still to come. Selah was amazed. It had only been a few days since he made the decision to follow a stranger, but now this man no longer felt like a stranger on this fantastic adventure. He felt he had aged years since that fateful night. He didn't feel like an unloved, unwanted boy anymore. He wasn't yet sure what he was, but he would find out soon enough.

Kaya went up to bed soon after their meal. She was so tired, she actually allowed Selah and Enoch to clean up. She had been up all day waiting for Selah at the bottom of the mountain where Kaya's people have lived for thousands of years guarding their precious charge. Kaya had seemed so ageless that Selah had almost forgotten that she was an elderly woman.

Selah considered the power of the Tablet and thought that if he had wanted to hide such a powerful object, the Hopi would be the perfect keepers for it. The Hopi, the peaceful people. He thought of the prophecy Kaya had revealed to him that showed the similarities with the Christian, Judaic, and Islamic prophecies of a messiah and the end of days. He knew this was no coincidence. There were no coincidences, not when one is able to see behind the veil and know the truth.

After the chores, Selah and Enoch sat on the couch drinking tea. It was delicious. After dinner, Selah had asked Kaya what it was. She had told him it was ginger tea. Selah had never had ginger tea before; he liked it. The two of them enjoyed their last night in this world. They would be leaving for the gate at sunrise.

Selah asked Enoch, "The Tablet of Destiny is the *Sefer Ha-Sefarim* isn't it? And the Staff of the Gods is the *Mateh Ha-Elohim*?" He thought he knew the answer, but he didn't want to lean on his own understanding, since that would be the fool's path. His grandfather used to read him the book of proverbs and counsel his grandson. *Never lean to your own understanding*, he would say. If this journey had taught Selah anything, it was that he didn't know anything at all.

"Yes," Enoch confirmed. "One of man's greatest fallacies along with the thought that they are alone is the idea that they worship different Gods. There is one Creator, *El Echad*, *Al Ahad*. He is the creator of all, all there was, is, and will be. He reveals Himself to those whose hearts are humble and those who can discern this one truth. He has many attributes and is known by many names. He revealed Himself to Abraham as *Shadai*, to Muhammad as Allah. As a soul ascends, he learns the true name. It is revealed to him so he may protect, lead, and teach the people as He did with Moshe.

To believe in an omnipresent, omniscient, and omnipotent God, and then think that anything can come from another source is illogical and the thoughts of a foolish man," he stated with passion. "The *Sefer* will bring balance to this realm and bring creation in alignment with the will of the Creator."

Selah's eyes were getting heavier. It had been a very long day. On seeing the young man's exhaustion, Enoch decided to end their conversation.

The weary travelers went off to their respective rests. Selah lay in the bed looking up at the moon through the window. It looked bigger and brighter. Selah recalled the night sky in his *Isra*. He didn't think he would ever see a night sky that would ever equal that sight. There was such wonder and beauty in this endless and limitless universe for a traveler to discover. He gently fell asleep, and as he left his body, he could have sworn he heard voices singing— a man and a woman singing a magical song, a song full of light and love.

Chapter Eight

At sunrise, Selah and Enoch said goodbye to Kaya. While Enoch packed the van—Kaya had given them more supplies—Selah and his new friend shared a quiet moment. Selah hadn't had many years with his mother and always felt he had missed out on something special. Meeting Saba and Kaya confirmed it. Enoch guided him, and protected him, but these women fed a part of him he had long ignored.

Kaya pulled the young man into her arms. She then kissed his forehead, looked into his eyes, and blessed him. "This is my blessing: May the light of the Blue Star guide your path and may Darkness bow before you." She pulled Selah back into her arms, afraid to let him go, though she knew he wasn't hers to keep. "My people have waited so long for you, keeping the old ways. We have lost so much, but now I know that our sacrifices have not been in vain. We will wait, and when the time is right, I will search the night sky for the Blue Star."

Selah fought tears as he held her. He held on to her as tightly as she was holding on to him. He had grown fond of her in the short time that he had spent with her. Her faith in him meant more than she had realized. Finally, Kaya pulled back and returned inside the house. She didn't turn back. Selah watched her disappear and felt the weight of all her hopes and dreams. He promised himself that he wouldn't let her or her people down.

"We must leave, we have miles to cover before we reach the gate, and we have things to discuss," Enoch informed his charge.

"I'm coming. Give me one minute," Selah replied.

The young man stood in the courtyard of the small abode and looked at the mountain in the early morning light. The sun was rising and illuminating the earth with its light. Too often people took these small wonders for granted. He had once taken these small wonders for granted himself. Now, Selah saw miracles and signs in everyday actions. He knew that divinity was hidden in the smallest things. The Most High wasn't some far-reaching presence, but right there with him, speaking to him in the wind, guiding him with the stars, nurturing him with the earth.

Selah considered how, being so far removed from the eternal, mankind thought they are separate from the universe. But they were not. Mankind's ignorance and ingratitude had made them unfit to inherit this realm. The Unseen wanted to depose the incompetent monarchy. Man was ungrateful, forgetful, and foolish, but that's what grace was. Grace was about giving indiscriminately, even to the undeserving. Selah had no clue how to defend mankind, but he guessed he would find out.

"We must prepare you for opening the gate," Enoch informed Selah as soon as they were on the road.

"How do I do that? We talked about it a little bit, and you mentioned that the *naars* can find the gate and open it. How?" Selah asked.

"Locating the gate is the easy part. The challenge is in opening it. The gatekeepers will open the gate when they are called to open it. As a lower being, you cannot open the gate at night, so we will have to wait until the sun is high for you to open it. The gate is located inside what the locals call *Zona Del Silencio*, the Zone of Silence. You must create the conditions for opening the gate, and then open it."

"Okay, how do I open it? What should I do?" Selah became increasingly frustrated and anxious.

"The gates function as the *Arbot*, they also have governors or, in this case, a keeper who governs those who pass. Different *arachs* or travelers use different gates and different words to open it. In the same manner as your modern airplanes. The passengers don't all sit in the same sections or receive the same amenities though they are all on the same aircraft. It depends on the ticket they present at the boarding gate.

"The king redeemed you during your *Isra*, he paid your ticket. When you were crossing, you received the *Birkat Ha-Melek*, the blessing of the king. In this case, you will not have it, and, therefore, must present your own ticket."

"What is my ticket? Do I have to pay the gatekeeper?"

"Not with money. You need to have the words to call the gatekeepers."

"What are the words? What should I say?"

"As I mentioned, each traveler has their own personal ticket identifying them specifically. Only you know what to say to open the gates. The words will come to you, we must trust that at the right time, the words will come to you."

"Faith," said Selah.

"Faith," echoed Enoch.

"What are the conditions that I need to create before speaking the words to open it?" asked Selah.

"You need to find a way to create a space that can be made sacred—a place to separate the holy from the mundane to facilitate the crossing."

"I don't understand," replied Selah.

"You would not go to a bus station to catch a plane, right? You would go to the airport," Enoch explained.

"I need to create the landing strip?" asked Selah in reply.

"Something to that effect," Enoch said.

Why weren't these things ever simple? Selah thought. Then made the statement out loud to his companion.

"On the Tree of Life, there are ten *Sephirot* that are revealed. The eleventh, *Daat,* is concealed, because knowledge must be sought after. The wise are not the ones who know everything, but those who know they know nothing, and seek after knowledge." Enoch informed his charge.

Although Selah wished wisdom was a little more accessible, he understood it would not be as precious if it were. "You know the answers, Selah, you have always known them. You simply have to remember what you already know." Enoch tried to assure the young man. But from the look on Selah's face, it didn't seem to be working. Selah's self-confidence had increased in the past week, but he still had lingering doubts. He still feared that he would not be enough. Enoch knew that there wasn't much he could do about Selah's inner struggle. That was one path a man had to walk alone, so he left the young man alone with his thoughts and concentrated on getting them across the border by nightfall.

A landing strip. How in the name of all that is holy was he supposed to build a landing strip for some celestial plane being piloted by magical beings? Selah thought. Feeling his fear coming back, he closed his eyes and tried to breathe. Everything they had been through depended on him opening the gate. Everything! Selah felt the weight of his responsibilities on his shoulders. With his eyes closed, he tried to control his breathing, but even to his own ears it sounded more like he was hyperventilating then consciously breathing.

"Easy." Enoch cautioned. He was becoming worried by the sounds coming from Selah.

With his eyes still closed, Selah tried to take control of his breathing, slowing it down and forcing his mind to think of something else. He knew the mind could be your best friend, but it could also be a terrifying and cruel master if given free reign. Selah started thinking about his grandfather, the most stable and stabilizing influence in his life.

Solomon Jacobi had spent countless hours with his grandson—teaching him, nurturing in him a love of books and knowledge. Selah thought about the times he had spent reading with his grandfather. Solomon's favorite book was, of course, the Tanakh. The old man knew every book in the Tanakh as though he had written it himself, and the Torah was the most beloved part for him. Selah let his thoughts drift as different scenes played out in his mind. He thought of the hours he had spent with his grandfather instructing him on the Laws, and telling him about the prophets, judges, and kings.

One of Solomon's favorite stories was of King Dawad buying the threshing floor of Arnan the Yebusite in order to save Yisrael. After Dawad had disobeyed Him, the Most High gave a word over Yisrael and 70,000 men fell. He then sent the Angel of Destruction with a sword to destroy Yerushalem. Out of compassion, the Most High haltered the Angel of Destruction and told him to stay his hand. The Angel of יהוה then informed the prophet Gad to tell Dawad to purchase the threshing floor of Arnan the Yebusite. Gad instructed Dawad to build an altar and to offer a sacrifice there. When Dawad tried to buy the property, Arnan offered it for free, but Dawad insisted on paying for it because he could not make a present to the Lord of what belonged to another or sacrifice an offering that cost nothing. It was on that spot that the Temple of Solomon was built.

As a child, Selah was fascinated by the imagery of valiant kings and angels with swords. Solomon's focus was different; he wanted Selah to understand the significance of the threshing floor and the importance of offerings. Solomon had told him that story more than once and always wanted him to remember what a threshing floor was used for: to separate the chaff from the grain, the worthy from the worthless, the holy from the mundane.

Selah opened his eyes, finally understanding the lesson his grandfather had tried to teach him. The threshing floor wasn't to harvest food for the body, but also for the soul. It was a symbol of separation, setting apart that which was holy from the mundane. Recalling an image in his mind of a threshing floor, he could also see its resemblance to the kiva. They were large circles in a flat elevated position. Selah smiled to himself. He knew what he needed to create in order to open the gate. He felt a moment of doubt and hesitated, but quickly quenched it. He felt it in his gut that it was the right thing to do. He knew it was. He had to learn to trust himself and his instincts. If Enoch, Kaya, and all the others believed in him, then it was time he started believing in himself.

The sun completed its circuit across the sky to its resting place by the time they had crossed the border into Mexico. They stayed on the back roads away from the main thoroughfare. Enoch drove the van like someone who had made the trip on a regular basis. After a week, Selah was still amazed by the surety and confidence the man used to navigate through life. He seemed so sure of everything. His faith in himself, life, and the universe was solid, unshakeable, untouchable, and incorruptible. Selah wanted to grow up and be just that kind of man.

A few hours after crossing, Enoch pulled off the road into an isolated camping area. He informed Selah that they would spend the night there and finish their journey in the morning. Selah's stomach tied up into knots. Though he had a plan and was almost positive it was the correct thing, he was still very nervous. He didn't know what to expect. What would it be like? Where would he go? What would happen? All the variables were running around in his mind. His imagination could not conjure up any scenarios. The events of the past few days had all been beyond anything his imagination could invent. After all, how does one envision the unknowable?

By the time Enoch had finished setting up their camp, Selah had become a bundle of raw nerves. He had felt that the smallest breeze would shatter him. He found himself pacing back and forth behind the van, getting in Enoch's way as he attempted to settle them for the night. Finally, unable to take the young man's anxiety, Enoch signed, "Selah, your thoughts are too loud. You are practically screaming at this point. Calm your thoughts. What is meant to happen has already happened. There is no point to your anxiety."

Selah halted his pacing, took a deep breath, and walked over to his mentor. Enoch pointed to one of the folding chairs he had set up for them. Selah took a seat and tried to focus his thoughts on the things he could control at the moment. He looked at Enoch and asked, "Is there anything I can do to help?"

"Can you gather some sticks for the fire?" Enoch asked. Selah quickly agreed, recognizing busy work when he saw it. Selah knew that Enoch could call fire at will and he did not need Selah to gather firewood. But this exercise in futility would keep him occupied, so Selah went off into the brush to gather the unnecessary items.

Selah became distracted with his task and walked further away from their camp. His mind had been overcome with possibilities of what could happen the next day and how he would create an opening for the gate. He hoped he was making the right decision. He became more aware of the environment when it became darker as he had walked further away from their firelight. Deciding that he had enough firewood, Selah turned around to return to Enoch. Just then he felt the hairs on the back of his neck rise up—the most instinctive and primal response of the prey when a predator is near.

His breath left his body when a voice, thick with malevolence, whispered to him, "You are a brave *naar*, indeed, to stray this far from the light, on a night such as this one." Selah felt something to his right as the being in the dark moved closer to him. He knew that voice, he had heard it somewhere before, but he wasn't sure where, or who it belonged to. He backed up from the voice and intended on running. The creature laughed. "You never run from a predator *naar*; it turns you into prey. Didn't your teacher teach you that?" Selah paused in his tracks, unsure of how to proceed. He watched as the figure came out of the shadows, it was Tsar-El, the adversary.

"Selah!" Enoch suddenly came crashing through the brush and took a stand behind him. Selah immediately felt relief in his mentor's presence. There was more movement on his left as an additional shadow formed. This one was larger and in the shape of a large bird with a wingspan of about six feet. Selah moved closer to Enoch as the shape congealed into a man taller than Enoch, with broad shoulders and a dark countenance.

"Enoch Ben Yared, the Scribe, the Prince of the world, the Youth, the Prince of the Presence." The second man could now be seen clearly as he was no longer a part of the surrounding darkness. He mocked a bow before Enoch, and continued, "This Enoch whose flesh was turned to flame, his veins to fire, his eyelashes to flashes of lighting, his eyeballs to flaming torches, and who the Most High placed on a throne next to the Throne of Glory. He who received after his heavenly transformation the name Meta—"

"Enough!" exclaimed Enoch. The man's laughter echoed through the night, as he walked ever closer. The two of them—Tsar-El, his adversary, and the other man who seemed particularly interested in Enoch—now stood opposite Selah and Enoch.

"It's been a while, Scribe, is it? Is that the title you are clinging to? Fair enough." And then he looked directly at Selah and said, "This must be the new lamb to the slaughter." His voice was so deep that Selah's innards vibrated with each word. Selah felt a shiver in his limbs. The minute the second man appeared, he had known that this was no man, but one of the angels. But this one was different, there was something else. Selah felt the same physical discomfort around him, but with this time, there was also fear caused by a certain malevolence. Selah knew that this man was not one of the beings made of light but of darkness.

"Do you know who your teacher is Ben Adam?" This question came from Tsar-El. "Did he tell you who he is? Did he tell you how many he has led to their deaths? Young man, the lesser in their home, the Mashiachs, the prophets he taught how to die, to die for his lost cause." Selah didn't answer, as he didn't really have one to give.

"Did he inform you that you will be dying tomorrow?" he asked with false concern.

Selah was hesitant to turn his gaze from Tsar-El, but he dared a quick look at Enoch to gauge his reaction to the statement. Enoch hadn't flinched, instead, he had stoically kept his eyes on the man standing across from him.

"What? Is Enoch the Mute one of your many titles, Scribe? Will you not defend yourself?" the man asked.

"One defends himself against false charges. Tomorrow is not promised to anyone," replied Enoch. Selah was surprised by his answer. They had never discussed the possibility of death. He would have remembered if "possible death" had been a part of their conversations. He wasn't going to contradict Enoch though. He didn't know who the other man was, but one thing he did know was that Enoch was the only one he could trust. So he dismissed Tsar-El's words.

The adversary looked at the young man, taking note of the resilient way he squared his shoulders. *Well what do you know*, he thought.

The man chuckled. "Always a brilliant reply, it's a shame, really, that you couldn't use your eloquence to defend me. Or was it because the charges against me were true?" Enoch made no reply but kept his eyes square on every shift and movement from the man.

Leaning forward, so close he could have kissed Enoch, the man sneered, "Do you have any idea how long I have been bound here? How offensive the smell of their perpetually decaying flesh is to me?" he asked Enoch.

"If memory serves me, your fondness for their flesh was the reason why you were bound to his realm," Enoch retorted.

"I should have been the only one to pay for my crime!" he shouted. With his shout, he became larger, and dark luminous wings sprouted and spread out across his back. The wind from the wings knocked Selah down. Selah could not believe his eyes—wings, heavens above, wings!

The man hovered a few inches off the ground. "Our children were murdered. We were bound! For eons, we were turned into flightless birds!" he raged. His voice boomed. Selah covered his ears and crouched on the shaking ground. The night sky trembled. *I am going to die tonight*, Selah thought.

"Why do they get second chances, receive grace and forgiveness for the weaknesses built into their character? Why do they get His love? We were created to err, to suffer! Then punished for following the plan. Why?

He slowly lowered himself to the ground. "You were supposed to speak for us, to requite grace for us, but, instead, you rendered His judgment on us! You get to be with Him, to leave this wretched realm, yet you too have committed atrocities."

Selah lifted his head and looked at Enoch. "Enoch?" he questioned.

The man laughed. "Did he not tell you that he was the Man clothed in linen with the inkhorn. Your mentor, *naar*, went around Yerushalem marking everyone for slaughter. Thousands died at His command, and you, Scribe, you signed their death certificates." He provided Selah the information with relish.

"I did as commanded, I will always do as commanded. I did not sentence you, nor do I have the power to. We both serve the same master," Enoch responded.

"And, yet, here we are on opposite sides." His wings retreated into his back and the air seemed less charged. Selah pulled himself to his knees, then slowly rose to his feet. He wasn't sure why the effect wasn't as bad this time around. Although he was still weak and unable to look him in the face, the trembling hadn't been as debilitating. He still hoped that the situation wouldn't turn violent. He wasn't sure he would be able to run if he had to.

"Sam—" Enoch began.

The man interrupted him, and shouted, "You don't get to say my name if I don't get to say yours!"

"You cannot interfere in this," continued Enoch.

"What?" The man touched his chest in mock innocence. "I am not interfering. "I just came to watch. That's all we do ... watch. He backed away from them and said in parting, "The day will come, Scribe, when you and I will come to terms. You, the First Prince, and I, we will come to terms."

"Yes," confirmed Enoch. "But not tonight."

Silence reigned after he had parted. Selah wasn't sure what to say to his mentor. This night had brought more than he had anticipated.

"Do you want to be standing next to him when the reckoning comes?" Tsar-El asked. "Are you willing to die for him? Those who watch can't touch you. But in the morning are you willing to face Qeteb and his force?" taunted Tsar-El.

"He will bring destruction. He was created to bring devastation and mayhem. You are a mere boy compared to beings who were created before the light. You are no one, nothing. Why take part in this fight? Leave and return to your life. In fact, you can have a new life—one with love, family, riches. What is he promising you other than certain death? A life of servitude to stiff-necked people, who refuse to bow their heads before their Creator? Leave. Go home. This man you are following will kill you if he is commanded to do so. How can you trust him? Go home, leave this place, and live in peace. You and yours will be long dead before the destruction of this world. Go home."

"I have no home. I have no other purpose than this. This was the reason why I was born. One doesn't feel the divine presence until one lives according to one's purpose," Selah humbly replied.

"Then you will die," Tsar-El stated with conviction.

"Then I will die," Selah replied with confidence.

Tsar-El searched Selah with his eyes, then turned around, and walked back into the darkness. He had blended into the night. Selah felt when he and Enoch were once again the only beings broadcasting their presence, the others chose to stay concealed behind the night's veil.

"Let us return to the campfire," Enoch suggested.

They walked back in silence. Selah noticed how far he had walked away from Enoch. That hadn't been his brightest moment. When they returned to their camp, the fire was already lit. The light seemed brighter than regular firelight. Selah suspected it was to deter any other resentful night beings. He was glad for it. He felt better now that they were away from their uninvited guests, but he didn't have the strength or energy for another confrontation.

Enoch prepared a humble repast for them. Selah suspected the food was really for him, because Enoch never seemed to get tired. Selah had so many questions, but he had one very pressing one which needed to be addressed first.

"Would you kill me if you were commanded to?" Selah knew the answer, but for some reason, he wanted to hear Enoch say it.

"Yes." Enoch confirmed.

"I would not like it, but yes, if commanded, I would. Selah, you must understand, even with all my knowledge and, yes, titles, I still don't know everything. This is the reason why I press upon you the importance of faith. You are a friend. You have become dear to me, but my purpose, while it includes you, is not you. There is a greater plan in the works; creation is revealing it itself. This is bigger than you or me, or any affection we might have developed for one another. I would gladly give my life for yours, and yes, I would take it as well if it were part of my master's plan. We are servants.

I might be able to call fire, bind spirits, and return life to flesh, but I didn't give fire its name, I didn't create the spirit, and life and death don't rest in my hands. My master rules all these things, including me. Real power, real strength lies in understanding this." Enoch quietly explained.

"I understand." Selah assured his friend. And he did. This was bigger than them. What they were tasked to do was for a far greater purpose.

"I cannot interfere between you and your adversary. His purpose is to oppose you, not me. That fight will always be between the two of you. Your strength of character, your will power, those are the weapons with which you can fight him. His task is to make you doubt your purpose. It is written in Muhammad's Holy Book that: *No bearer of burdens shall bear the burden of another. And if one heavily laden calls another to bear his load, nothing of it will be lifted even though he is near kin,*" said Enoch in a quiet voice.

"I figured that out for myself. It was pretty obvious," Selah said with a cheeky smile.

"Has the student outgrown the teacher?" Enoch joked with the young man.

"Not even close," Selah rejoined. They both chuckled, releasing the tension that was in the air.

Enoch sobered up and said, "Selah, tomorrow will be a fight. There were no lies uttered this evening. We will not be alone though. Qeteb will bring his legion tomorrow, and we will bring our own."

Chapter Nine

This is it, Selah thought upon waking in the morning. This was the day he had been working his way towards since he had started this journey a week ago. No, this was the moment his early childhood had prepared him for, this was the reason he had been born. After a quiet breakfast and quickly refreshing himself in a nearby bush, the young man walked over to his contemplative mentor. Enoch had been silent for most of the morning, and Selah had left him to his thoughts.

"So, it's game day. What is our plan?" Selah was nervous, but he refused to let his fear paralyze him, not today.

"We take the rest of the way on foot. We are close to the Mapimi Biosphere. We should have visitors once we get closer to the Zone of Silence. Selah, you cannot physically fight any of them. That is not your task. Your task is to open the gate, just that. Keep your head down, keep moving until you can see the veil."

"The veil?"

"You will know it when you see it. It is a thick demarcation separating this realm from the *arba*—the crossings where we can travel from one realm to the other. The gatekeepers must open the gate. They will only do so if your words bring them forth. The gate will not open until the day is high. This gives our adversaries plenty of time to dissuade us from our goal."

"How are the two of us supposed to withstand an army of supernatural beings for any amount of time?" Selah appreciated the power of positive thinking, but this was just plain ridiculous.

"Two of us? Maybe you should look again." Enoch smiled.

Selah had been facing Enoch. As the sun rose from the east, a large shadow loomed over their figures. The shadow was in the shape of a large being with a far-reaching wingspan. Selah watched as Shamar-Yah landed soundlessly on the ground. His wings were different from the man last night. His wings were made of pure shining light. Selah's mouth dropped open in unadulterated joy and awe. One by one, the others appeared out of thin air, with their wings majestically spread out, blocking the rising sun from Selah's eyes. Selah thought the sight of his guardians was blinding, but he was left completely awestruck as one by one more beings walked out of the desert. Each came down to earth like bolts of lighting, wings open, light surrounding them, covering them in glory and grace. Never in his life had he thought he would ever see such a sight. There were hundreds of them. Hundreds. Heaven's host of hundreds bending the clouds to come to his aid. Seeing the look on the young man's face, Shamar-Yah reiterated, "You are not *Nobody*."

Selah felt the tears pool in his eyes as he remembered his words. Once he had felt so alone, so lost. Now, he stood with Heaven's hosts preparing to defend him so he could fulfill a destiny his mind could have never imagined. *My grandfather would have loved this moment*, the young man thought. His guardians surrounded him and Enoch. Another thirty or so formed a larger circle around the group. Selah noticed the delineation between them and the others.

"Who are they?" he asked no one in particular.

"They are the Thirty and Three, your *giborim*," Enoch stated. "You might say they are your own personal army. They will follow your command one day. For now, they are here to make sure that you live long enough to command them." Selah found Enoch's statement a bit daunting. But he had been reassured by their presence. He knew they were about to face an army bent on stopping him from crossing over.

"Selah, we have to get moving, we are burning daylight." Selah went to the van and grabbed his backpack. Last night he had made sure he had placed his mother and grandfather's pictures in the bag, along with the blanket from Kaya. He had left the Staff next to the bag, but now, on a hunch, he put the Staff in the bag too, and it fit in completely. He left everything else in the van. He wouldn't need worldly things anymore. He tightened the straps of his backpack, taking a final look around, really seeing this world, he filled his lungs with air, feeling them expand. He enjoyed the simple act of drawing breath. He closed his eyes, feeling the breeze brushing across his skin. It was such a simple pleasure but one that he wasn't sure when, if ever, he would enjoy again. "Selah?" Selah took another fortifying breath, opened his eyes, and walked towards Enoch. The two of them along with their hosts started across the desert.

Selah wondered at the picture they made—Enoch, he, and their small army. He estimated that they were accompanied by three hundred men including the Thirty and Three. He imagined that if a passerby saw them, they would only be able to see him and Enoch. Perhaps not even Enoch. Maybe all they would see would be a young black male walking in the desert. The thought made him chuckle. Humans tended to do that, to measure someone too quickly based on their own history, only relying on what they perceived with their five senses. He thought of the famous quote from Shakespeare: "*There are more things in heaven and earth, than are dreamt of in your philosophy.*" Shakespeare had no clue how much more was in the heavens and the earth.

They had been walking for most of the morning when Selah finally saw the sign *Zona Del Silencio*, the Zone of Silence. But it wasn't the sign that had the group stop in their tracks. It was the army falling down from the heavens to welcome them. Selah's heartbeat quickened. He had been impressed by the size of his group, but his adversaries seemed to be more than double in numbers. There had to be thousands of winged beings standing in opposition.

Selah watched in dread as they sheathed their wings and unsheathed their swords. Far worse than the swords was the appearance of these creatures. They didn't all have the likeness of men. Most of the creatures were fanged. Hundreds of them had bodies covered in scales, with long talons, poisonous-looking fangs, and forked tongues. They resembled large reptiles more than people. While others resemble large hairy dogs on all fours with dripping fangs, chopping at the bit. They were all waiting for the command to attack. Selah's brain quickly tried to process the horror that besieged his sight.

"It is written: I will send the teeth of beasts upon them, with the poison of serpents of the dust." Selah whispered, terrified.

Uri-Yah moved in front of him and countered, "It is written: Thou shalt not be afraid of the terror by night, nor the arrow by day."

Uzzi- El took his position at his right and continued, "Nor of Pestilence who walks in darkness, nor of Destruction who lays waste at noonday."

Shamar-Yah on his left confirmed, "A thousand shall fall at thy side, and ten thousand at thy right hand. It will not draw near thee."

At his back Hannah-El assured him, "Only with thy eyes, shall thou observe it. And you will see the requital of the evil ones."

Walking to the lead of the group, Enoch turned and met Selah's eyes. "For you have made the Most High your refuge, no evil shall befall you." As a single unit the group moved towards their enemies.

When they were a few yards away, they stopped, and Selah watched as two men separated themselves from the pack. They were tall and dressed in armor. Their swords were almost the length of Selah's entire body. These were beings built for war and devastation. They were vastly different from the ones Selah had met so far. It wasn't only because of the fact they were the first beings who seemed to be made for the daytime, it was the general energy about them, it was aggression in its purest form. These men were "war". The one on the right looked as if he were a weapon, like his entire purpose was to kill, the other slightly shorter one reminded Selah of a boulder. His complexion matched that of the desert sand, and he seemed camouflaged by the surroundings.

"Who are they?" Selah asked no one in particular.

"Chets and Qeteb," replied Uri-Yah.

"Enoch, the Seventh from Adam!" shouted the one who resembled the desert boulders. "Is this all you could muster? Does not 'the Scribe Who Ministers to the Throne' command a larger army? I am disappointed. I thought 'He who on his own account carries out the Word to the world' would offer me a challenge."

"Qeteb," acknowledged Enoch.

Enoch's slight made his mark. He had not heralded Qeteb's name, nor acknowledged his authority or fame. He simply spoke to him as "Qeteb" a foot soldier, no one of consequence. The sneer on Qeteb's face turned into a snarl.

"Um… Enoch are you trying to enrage the angry boulder? He had looked ready to eat us before, but, now, he looks like he will enjoy it," Selah whispered to Enoch.

"He knows what he is here to do. You have a mission, stay focused. Remember: you cannot fight them. Your aim is to make it to the signpost. Can you see the veil next to it?" Enoch spoke softly to Selah but kept his eyes on Qeteb and his army of ghouls.

Selah looked over Qeteb's shoulder to the *Zona Del Silencio* sign. He let his eyes lose their focus, and then, there it was—a shimmer, the way the horizon looks when one is driving on a hot day, a ripple in the air a few feet behind the sign. "Yes," Selah replied.

"That is your destination. Our job is to get you across this field in one piece. Whatever happens, do not stop moving. Do you understand? I have walked this earth longer than you can imagine. I am much more than what you see. Do not concern yourself about me. Are we clear?" At Selah's hesitation, Enoch took his eyes away from Qeteb long enough to search the young man's face.

"Are we clear?" he repeated.

"We are clear." Selah responded. "This is a game of football, and I am the ball," he joked.

"That's the spirit." Enoch smiled with pride in his charge. The young man had come a long way from the boy that he had met a week ago. Enoch returned his gaze to their adversaries. In a loud voice he stated, "Yakum *Elohim yafu tzu oy'vayhu, w-yanusu m'sanayhu m'panayhu*! Let Elohim rise, let his enemies be scattered. Let them that hate him flee from before him." It was a battle cry, plain and simple. Both sides responded to it by charging towards each other. Selah felt the ground shake as the armies ran towards each other— the *giborim* created to defend the Chosen of the Throne against Destruction and his minions. Selah ran with the group. He felt more than heard Shamar-Yah say, "I am with you, just run, I will handle all who strive against you." Selah ran.

He didn't get very far. The swarm of creatures attacked them full force. They were surrounded. Selah was entrenched by the *giborim* and his guardians. Shamar-Yah was the closest to him, his wings shielded Selah from every strike. Seeing an opening in the melee, Selah slipped through and took off for the veil.

A cracking sound came from his right. As he looked, Selah saw the ground form into a boulder. And that boulder flew towards his head. Throwing himself to the ground, Selah covered his head and felt the skin on his knuckles get scraped off. The sting only served to motivate him. Rising to his feet, he looked around to reorient himself and sped off towards the sign. "Selah!" Hearing his name being shouted, he instinctively turned around and then wished he hadn't. One of the serpentine creatures was gunning for him. The beast animal was moving so fast that Selah knew he could never outrun it. He tried anyway. Selah pumped his legs and ran towards the sign. Selah felt and smelt the creature's breath at the back of his neck. He wasn't going to make it. Pure stubbornness made Selah feign to the right. The creature leapt for him and missed him by inches. Instead it crashed into one of the furry doglike beasts, which turned its jaw and ripped off the head of the serpentine creature. Selah gagged on the stench but kept running.

Another one of the creatures almost reached him but, at the last minute, one of the *giborim* crashed into the creature. Their impact threw Selah into the ground. Selah watched as the *giborim* grabbed the creature's jaw and tore his head open in two pieces. He got up, threw the carcass to the ground and jumped right back into the fray.

Selah's knuckles were bleeding, but he didn't have time to triage the damage. Once again, getting off the ground, he barreled forward towards his goal. He hadn't taken two steps before he was hit. Hard. At first, he thought it was a boulder, but when his hands touched his attacker, he realized it was a tail. He had gotten so close that one of the serpentines was able to hit him with its tail. The creature swung its tail and hit him again—the second strike—and lifted him straight off the ground. Selah landed on the ground and heard his ribs crack. The young man laid on the ground cradling his ribs. Everything hurt. The pain spread throughout his entire body. There was a wet sensation in the back of his head. Selah suspected it was blood from his landing. He opened his eyes and realized that his vision was blurred. He touched the back of his head and looked at his hands. His suspicion was confirmed, it was blood.

"Selah!" He heard Enoch's voice in the fracas, and he tried to get up. He shook his head in an attempt to clear his vision. It hurt. A lot. But it helped clear it up. Focusing his eyes, he could see Shamar-Yah running towards him. The angel was fighting his way towards him, all the *giborim* were. Selah got to his knees, then his feet. He searched for Enoch in the middle of the carnage. When he spotted his mentor, Selah was strengthened by his presence, and finally managed to steady himself. That's when the ground trembled, cracked open, and Selah felt himself falling into the depth of the earth.

"Selah!"

He heard the desperation in Enoch's voice. It was the first time since he knew him that Selah had ever heard fear in his mentor's voice. He tried to reach for purchase as the fissure in the ground increased and he fell. His fingers touched and scraped the ground as he fell. He threw his weight to the side, only to have his head strike the wall, but still he fell. His battered head now had matching bleeding wounds in the front and the back.

Selah looked up as he fell, and the light dimmed. He thought it was due to the head wounds, but then realized the sun was being blocked by a large figure. On instinct, he reached out his hand and felt a strong hand grab his wrist. He felt the strong breeze as Shamar-Yah beat his wings to lift them from the subsidence. Once they cleared the opening, Shamar-Yah was immediately attacked by one of the doglike creatures.

The creature leapt into the air and collided with them. Shamar-Yah threw Selah away from the assault. Selah flew into the air into the arms of Uri-Yah. His relief was short-lived as Uri-Yah was attacked from behind by one of the serpentine creatures. At the last minute, before hitting the ground, Uri-Yah also threw the Selah volley to Hannah-El who caught him and gently placed Selah on the ground. The angel deftly manifested his sword in time to sever the furry head that was opening over his shoulder. Standing, he turned to face the approaching creatures. Selah looked for Enoch and saw him fighting Chets. The man looked small in comparison. Selah tried not to focus on his friend and returned his focus to his own task.

He was once again surrounded by the guardians, for the exception of Uzzi-El who was engaged in combat with Qeteb. Selah realized the combatants were slowly making their way to his location. Enoch and Uzzi-El were keeping Chets and Qeteb away from him, giving him time to get to the veil. Selah then searched for the signpost. He released a relieved breath when he realized that he was closer to it, maybe just a yard. A yard. Mustering all the strength left in his body, the young man got to his feet and limped towards the sign. As he moved, so did the *giborim* who somehow managed to converge on him and surround him. Selah remembered one of his grandfather's quotes from the book of psalms: "As the mountains surround Yerushalem, so יהוה surrounds His people from now until forever."

He was hurting everywhere. His knuckles were on fire, there was blood running down his face obscuring his vision which was already blurry from a probable concussion. But he kept moving. Selah held on to his ribs with one hand and kept placing one leg in front of the other. "Follow your feet," his grandfather would have said. So, he did. He followed his feet, and his faithful hosts followed him, keeping themselves between him and death.

The sound of Qeteb's enraged roar reverberated through Selah's body. The ground shook, and Selah hoped it didn't crack again. Another hit and he would not be able to get back up. That fear propelled him further and motivated him to move faster. The battle around him raged on, as fierce as the battle inside of him. The pain was whispering for him to rest, to give up. The pain told him he wasn't good enough, strong enough. He was "nobody," nothing, that he should just give up. But he followed his feet and pushed his body past its breaking point. Selah took a chance and looked up to see how far he had come. There it was. He could see shimmer, three feet, two, one. With the last of his strength, Selah launched his body. As he slipped through the shimmer, he heard a roar.

Selah lay on the ground. He was laying down on the ground with his backpack still strapped to his back underneath him. He was shocked the thing hadn't snapped off during the fight. He made it past the veil, but it wasn't done. With more strength than he knew he possessed, the young man lumbered to his feet. He unstrapped the backpack from his back and removed the Staff. The sound of the battle was muffled, but Selah could still hear it, as the warriors held back the horde bent on his destruction. He would not fail.

Selah dropped the backpack and limped further into the desert, past the veil. The desert looked the same, but everything looked sharper, the sun brighter. Selah took the Staff and slowly traced a large circle on the floor, the entire time hoping to bring the gatekeepers to his "threshing floor." He heard a large crack and felt the earth rumble. Selah stopped and looked for his friends. They were still locked in battle. "Keep going!" Enoch shouted. Selah followed the sound of his voice and saw him battling two of the creatures. One serpentine and another doglike. *Where was Qeteb?* Selah wondered. He worriedly searched for him but could not see him. The battle was now pressing closer to the veil. Selah wasn't sure if they were allowed to cross it, but he could not spend his time thinking about it.

Selah finished with his "threshing floor" and entered the circle. The sun had risen and was now at its zenith. The sun had risen behind him, so he knew it was right; "the gate facing east" was the one he needed. The gates would not be open until the sun was hot, which it was. This was it.

In the car on the way, Selah had realized what needed to be done. His grandfather had unknowingly taught him what he would need to do. In the Miqra it was written: "When the prince provides a freewill offering—whether a burnt offering or a peace offering voluntarily. Then the gate facing east is to be opened to him."

Selah stood inside the circle with the sun high above his head and offered the only thing he had to give—himself. He raised his hands to the sky with his palm facing him. "*Hineni.* Here I am," he said.

"I have nothing to offer but myself." As he stood there, the blood dripped from his forehead, slid down his arm, and quenched the parched desert sand.

Selah remembered the words and now uttered them as it is written. "Open to me the gates of righteousness. I will go into them and I will praise Yah. This gate of יהוה into which the righteous shall enter. I will praise thee for thou hast heard me, and art become my salvation. The stone which the builders refused has become the head stone of the corner. Blessed is he who comes in the name of יהוה."

A hush fell. The silence was deafening. Selah felt like he entered an electromagnetic field. Every strand of hair on his body was standing at attention. Then the heavens opened. Above his head a shimmery circle started to materialize. It grew and bent down until Selah was standing a few feet away from a swirling vortex of light. Selah couldn't hear any sound of fighting, so he turned to see what was happening with the battle. They were all standing completely still.

The creatures had their faces to the ground, the men, including his *giborim* all stood with their heads bowed down. Enoch and the guardians walked through the veil and stood inside Selah's circle. "Why aren't they attacking anymore?" asked Selah.

"Because weapons are not allowed at the gates of Tsion," replied Enoch, his eyes fixed on the opening gate.

. Selah looked at the light as it became brighter and two beings walked out of the vortex. They were beautiful, tall, taller than even the guardians. They were muscular and dressed in some kind of white material. With wings of light spread out behind them, they walked and stood at the entrance to the gate. The two beings faced each other and kneeled, extending their wings until the tips touched each other. The wings formed a tunnel. Selah stood transfixed, looking towards the passage created by the wings. There he could see the cosmos. All the stars, the planets, the universe mapped out, displayed before him.

Selah felt tears slide down his face. Tears of joy, of relief. He had done it. He was standing, his shoulders shaking with his sobs, at the gate of his destiny. Enoch grabbed his shoulders and said, "Well done."

Selah smiled a heartfelt smile. All the aches and pains were gone. Everything he had gone through in his life was for this very moment. Selah could now see it all. Everything fell into place. Every experience was purposeful and created for the fulfillment of this moment—his birth mother leaving him in the trash next to the hospital where his adoptive mother worked; Sharon, the daughter of a *shomrim*, finding him; Solomon's lack of a son, his love, and guidance. Even his mother and grandfather's death. They all made sense. Every event, loss, pain, had led him here to this gate. The gate through which the righteous would enter.

"Are you ready?" Enoch asked him.

Selah remembered Enoch asking him the same question that first night. Just like that night, he knew the question was not a simple one. Staring at the gate and the universe, Selah knew he was ready. Ready to face whatever came next. "I'm ready," he replied. Enoch walked in under the canopy of the gatekeepers' wings, vanishing in a burst of light. Selah stooped down and picked up a handful of dirt. He opened his palm and watched the wind blow the dust into the air. He made a full circle, took a final look around, took a breath and followed Enoch through the gate, vanishing in a burst of light. The desert settled herself back down. A gentle breeze swept through the dry desert sand.

Epilogue

The cool desert wind blew softly across the bronze skin of the tall man. He was an arresting man. He had strong shoulders, a stubborn tilt to his chin, and the lower half of his face was covered by a short beard. Anyone who saw him would automatically notice him. He was not the kind of person one would describe as non-descript. His features were too bold, too strong, and magnetic. But while he would be the center of attention in any situation, his gaze was towards the bright blue star in the sky.

Though the moon shone brightly in the sky, it could not hold a candle to that star.

The desert welcomed him home. It had been a very long time since he had been in this world. No one who knew him back then lived anymore. He had been a child the last time he had stood in this desert. A broken, hurt child, who had been chosen for a task most men would have failed. He hadn't. His destiny had long been written in the celestial books.

His destiny was revealed to him. While he had knowledge of what was to come, it hadn't all been revealed to him. Over a century before, he had made a choice based on faith. He chose to follow the path that would lead him here, to this desert, on this night, guided by that bright blue star. Once again, he chose to walk by faith and not by sight. In the darkness of the night, he had no fear. No fear of the dark, for as he stood in the desert, Darkness knelt down before him. He knew its name.

He knelt down and grabbed a handful of sand. He repeated the same gesture he had performed years before and opened his palm. He watched the wind blow the sand from his hand, and smiled. He took a deep breath, enjoying the feel of his lungs expanding and contracting. There was a simple kind of joy in the act. It had been a very long time since he had to function in this manner. He missed it. Looking around he realized the beauty of this realm. Why hadn't he noticed the fragrances of the wind before? How good it felt to have it rustle his clothing. He noticed all these things now. He understood how they all worked together for the glory of the Most High. He searched the horizon. He noticed the changes in the environment. The land felt different, bereft, lost. Things had gotten far worse since he had left. There was a strange feeling he could not name. Something else was in the air. It felt out of place. He took another breath and tasted the air. Yes, something was eating away at the world. He knew the time had come for man to be redeemed. They were lost, and creation was out of order. It was his task to put things back in alignment to free people who didn't even know they were imprisoned. He shouldered his backpack and set out once again in the world of men.

***

Unaware that his life was about to change, Raphael woke up to the shrill cry coming from his grandmother.

"Raphael!"

Raphael groaned when he heard his grandmother call his name. He loved his abuela, but sometimes the old woman could be a real pest. He had been having the best dream— Lina and he were dancing under the stars. She was in his arms and he couldn't have been happier.

"Raphael!"

"Coming, abuela!" the man answered.

Raphael had moved his grandmother in with him after the deaths of his parents. His wife, Lina, had died giving birth to their son. He named him Miguel after his father. He had to bury Miguel next to his mother less than a week later. He had the pleasure of being a husband for a year and a father for a week.

He stretched one last time and got out of bed. The sun hadn't fully risen, but his grandmother was usually up before the sun. He washed up and went out into the kitchen where he knew she would be. She was always in the kitchen. He walked over and kissed her round brown cheeks. He loved his grandmother. She was his only living relative. It was more than that though. The two of them have always been close. There was a connection there, one that didn't require definition. It simply was. After the death of his family, Raphael was sure he would have lost his mind if it hadn't been for his grandmother.

Luna smiled when she felt her grandson walk into the kitchen. She moved over to the table and poured his coffee. She had doted on him all his life. He was her only surviving grandchild. The two of them had buried all their loved ones together and were now inseparable. Raphael sat at the table and after the first sip asked her, "What do you need, abuela?"

"I am out of *reina de la noche*, and I need you to head out near the *Zona* to get me some more."

"Abuela, I got you some last week. How can you already be out?" he asked in surprise.

"Senora Montes is fighting a losing battle with old age and has been buying my potions. We need the money. Besides, she has been telling her friends about it. This is a good thing, Rapha," she said, patting him on the back. Raphael knew from past experiences that he would be knee-deep in cactus plants by midday. There was no point in arguing with Luna when she got an idea into her head. Raphael shook his head and finished his breakfast. He was going to need his strength today. Luna walked out of the kitchen and packed a small lunch and water for her grandson. She knew the boy was going to go get her the ingredients for her potions. He didn't believe in any of her mumbo jumbo as he called it, but he loved her so he would do it. The thought made her smile as it usually did whenever she thought of him.

Raphael and Luna lived on a small farm outside of what was once called Durango, Mexico. There weren't many people alive who still remembered that name. There weren't too many people alive who remembered the old ways, period. Luna was a great historian. She had taught him about his culture and the old ways of his people. When he was a child, those stories meant the world. His entire childhood was paved by his grandmother's stories. After he finished his breakfast, he grabbed the pack his grandmother prepared and left for the desert.

Luna was a medicine woman. She made different potions for the local people. People came to the farm for cures for everything from headaches to fertility issues. He wasn't a believer in Luna's cures, but then again, he didn't believe in anything anymore. Life had taken too much from him. He understood Luna's clients though. He understood their need to believe in something. Anything. In the last two centuries, the world has witnessed unprecedented technological advances. Sadly, Raphael felt those advances didn't include human development.

At first everybody saw the changes as benefiting the world. They were convenient, efficient, and exciting. By the time people realized how invasive the technologies had become, it was too late. They had all systematically given away sovereignty of their minds, and later on, their bodies. Raphael touched the scar on his shoulder where his chip had been. It had cost him everything he owned to pay for the removal, but it was worth it. He was free.

So, now, he lived in the middle of nowhere with his grandmother, a self-proclaimed *bruja*. Raphael laughed at the thought as he walked to the back of the house. He removed the cloth covering of the old machine. It was an antique. It once belonged to his grandmother's grandfather. It was the only thing of real value on the farm. Raphael had held on to it for two main reasons. The first was because the old thing worked. It was the main source of transportation for him when he needed to go to town for supplies, or to the desert for his grandmother's ingredients. The second reason was less pragmatic. He had kept it because it reminded him that life hadn't always been this bleak.

Once upon a time, man had deep thoughts. They had believed in God and goodness. There were places where the land was green, water was abundant, and the earth prospered. Once upon a time, women didn't die in childbirth and babies thrived. Now, life hung by a thread, and mankind no longer believed in anything.

Raphael started the ancient machine and drove out of the farm. He drove with the window open; he loved the feel of the wind on his face. Honestly, he didn't mind those excursions into the desert. It gave him a chance to be alone. Raphael loved being alone. The only company he cared for was Luna's; everyone else could go to hell. When he had decided to come out here with Luna, he had turned his back on the world. It had taken all he could give; he had nothing left they could take. He knew he was bitter, but he didn't care. What was the point of hope and love, life would just kill it, anyway?

Raphael drove and hummed an old song under his breath. He didn't know the words but had heard Luna hum it while she cooked. A movement on his left caught his eye. Raphael slowed the vehicle down to a stop when he saw a man walk out of the desert. He couldn't believe his eyes. As the man got closer, Raphael could see his face. He was tall, bearded, with broad shoulders, and he carried a beat-up backpack. In his right hand he held a staff.

The man stopped just a few feet away from Raphael's vehicle. Raphael got out of the vehicle and walked around until he stood a couple of feet from the man. The two men weighed each other silently for a beat before Raphael broke the silence. "Are you lost, sir?"

"No. I am exactly where I need to be." The man smiled and answered.

"I am Raphael, who are you?" Raphael wasn't sure why he was talking to this man. Usually, he would go out of his way to avoid people. But there was something about this man. He couldn't quite put his finger on it, but the man felt familiar.

"I was once called by a different name. You can call me Yadid Ben Solomon."

"Can I help you?"

"No, Raphael. I am here to help you," Yadid replied. Raphael felt a shift in the air, and in his chest. This was a momentous occasion. He didn't know why or how, but he knew that this meeting was going to change his life. This man was going to change his life. This man was going to change the world.